Switched at Birthday

Also by Natalie Standiford

The Secret Tree

The Boy on the Bridge

Confessions of the Sullivan Sisters

How to Say Goodbye in Robot

Switched at Birthday

Natalie Standiford

Scholastic Press / New York

Library of Congress Cataloging-in-Publication Data

Standiford, Natalie, author.
Switched at birthday / Natalie Standiford. — First edition.
pages cm
Summary: Lavender sees herself as the miserable but tough outsider at school, while Scarlet knows she is talented and popular, but insecure on the inside — then, on their mutual thirteenth birthday, they wake up in each other's bodies and are forced to learn what it means to walk in someone else's shoes.
ISBN 978-0-545-34650-4 (jacketed hardcover) 1. Identity (Philosophical concept) — Juvenile fiction. 2. Change (Psychology) — Juvenile fiction. 3. Magic — Juvenile fiction. 4. Birthdays — Juvenile fiction. 5. Friendship — Juvenile fiction. 6. Middle schools — Juvenile fiction. [1. Identity — Fiction. 2. Change (Psychology) — Fiction. 3. Magic — Fiction. 4. Birthdays — Fiction. 5. Friendship — Fiction. 6. Middle schools — Fiction. 7. Schools — Fiction.] I. Title.
PZ7.S78627Swi 2014
813.54 — dc23
2013018598

10 9 8 7 6 5 4 3 2 1   14 15 16 17 18

Printed in the U.S.A.   23
First edition, March 2014

The text type was set in Sabon MT.
Book design by Nina Goffi

To my parents:

I wouldn't switch for all the world.

Prologue
A Little Bit of Birthday Magic

Once there was a boy who lived in Kalamazoo, Michigan. His father was a baker and his mother was a candle-maker. They owned the Cake and Candle Company of Kalamazoo.

The cakes and candles that the boy's family made were perfectly ordinary in every way but one: When, on your birthday, you lit a Kalamazoo candle on a Kalamazoo cake and made a wish, a tiny spark of magic was ignited. And, if the stars were properly aligned, your birthday wish came true. But the magic only worked until you turned eighteen. After that, you had to make your birthday wishes come true on your own.

On his first birthday the boy wished for the ability to speak. After blowing out his candle, he said his first word: "Birfday."

On his fifth birthday the boy wished for a guitar, and when he opened his presents, there it was — the most beautiful boy-sized guitar he'd ever seen.

On his tenth birthday the boy wished he could sing a

solo with his school choir. His wish was granted the very next day, when the choir director chose him to sing "Jingle Bell Rock" in the Christmas pageant.

On his fifteenth birthday the boy wished to get a part in the school musical, *Camelot*. A week later he was cast as King Arthur.

And so it went, until his eighteenth birthday. That morning his mother said, "Remember, this is the last year that the birthday magic will work. Wish very carefully."

All day long the boy thought about what to wish for. That night, when his cake and candle were presented to him, he made a magic wish for the last time.

He wished for the ability to make magic for other people.

As always, his wish came true.

The next day, he got a letter from the Peabody Institute, a famous music school in Baltimore, Maryland, offering him a scholarship. So the boy from Kalamazoo got on a bus to Baltimore. For four years he studied music and drama at the Institute. He learned all about the magic of the theater. When he graduated he became a theater arts teacher.

And he never forgot how useful a little bit of birthday magic could be.

I

Lavender Blue

I didn't expect much of anything to happen on my thirteenth birthday. So I had been born. So what? Why should it be different from any other Monday?

The first twelve years, eleven months, and thirty days of my life had taught me not to get my hopes up.

When I got to school Maybelle Dawson galloped up and gave me a package wrapped in pale purple — otherwise known as *lavender* — paper. Maybelle Dawson was my best friend. Okay, my only friend.

"Happy birthday, Schmitzy!" she said.

My full name is Lavender Myrtle Schmitz. That's right: Lavender. Myrtle. Schmitz. Maybelle knew I hated *Lav* (slang for *bathroom* in the U.K., which meant I could never, ever set foot in England), so Maybelle called me Schmitzy. It made my mother weep.

Maybelle was very pretty, with curly hair and bright blue eyes and round rosy cheeks. But she had big hands and long flat feet and she *gallumphed* when she walked, and I guess that was enough to exile her to Loserville. My situation was more obvious: short hairy cavegirl + glasses = loser.

I was used to it.

"Open your present," Maybelle said. I ripped off the tissue paper. Inside was a framed picture of me playing my ukulele at the Falls Road Middle School Talent Extravaganza. Maybelle had made the frame herself, decorating it with tiny cardboard ukes and sprigs of lavender.

"Thank you, Maybelle," I said. "Thank you for memorializing one of the worst moments of my life. This way I'll never be tempted to perform in public again."

Her face clouded, and I immediately felt sorry. Words just blurped out of my mouth.

"I thought you were great that night," Maybelle said. "You should have won first prize."

At the Talent Extravaganza, against my better judgment, I'd gotten up in front of the entire school and sang the Hawaiian pop song "Tiny Bubbles," accompanying myself on the uke. I'd practiced for months, and by the day of the show I thought I sounded pretty decent. I waited backstage for my turn, watching the other acts. Most of the girls sang Taylor Swift songs or danced to hip-hop music. One boy did a magic act that no one seemed to like.

The more I watched, the more nervous I got. "Tiny Bubbles" was a terrible song choice. None of my classmates would know it. I should have picked something more popular — or at least something from this century.

My hands got sweaty and shaky. My face felt hot. When Mr. Brummel, our music teacher and the MC for the evening, called out my name, I barely recognized it.

If my feet hadn't felt nailed to the floor, I would have run home in a panic. Instead I found myself standing on the stage, alone in the spotlight, clutching my uke. I started to play "Tiny Bubbles." My voice was quavery. My fingering was unsure. I sounded nothing like I had in my bedroom.

I botched it.

And I was booed off the stage.

"I think this is a great picture of you," Maybelle said to me now.

It wasn't. There was no such thing as a great picture of me. "You meant well," I said.

John Obrycki walked up and looked at the picture. I put it away.

"Is today your birthday?" he asked. "If I'd known, I would have gotten you something."

"No, you wouldn't have," I said. We weren't friends, exactly. Though I supposed he was one of the less repulsive people at our school.

"Here," John said. "How's this?" He ripped a page out of his notebook and folded the paper into an origami star.

"Wow," I said. "That's really cool that you can make generic presents for people in about two seconds, without having to think about it or anything."

John's cheek twitched slightly.

"Schmitzy!" Maybelle elbowed me to let me know I was being rude. I didn't know why I'd said such a rude thing to John. Because I actually thought the star was pretty.

"Thank you," I said to John, putting the star with my hideous picture.

A loud burst of laughter came from across the hall. Scarlet Martinez glanced over the crowd at me, then looked away.

The problem with Falls Road Middle School was that it was "middle" in more ways than one. It was the middle between elementary school and high school, obviously. But it also sat right on the border of two very different neighborhoods: Hampden and Roland Park. Hampden was row houses and thrift stores and hipsters and ladies in curlers who called everyone "hon." Roland Park was big houses and big trees and preppies with fancy cars. I lived in Hampden, of course. Scarlet Martinez and her friends mostly lived in Roland Park.

Scarlet had long, wavy hair and long, long legs and big hazel eyes. She was skinny, but not too skinny. Whatever she wore was always the perfect thing to wear. She was good at soccer. She seemed to be good at everything. I wished just once she'd do something awkward and make a fool of herself. But she never did. She was surrounded by a crowd of the most popular kids, the Glossy Posse and their boy followers.

The floor at Scarlet's feet was littered with wrapping paper. Someone had brought a box of cupcakes and Scarlet's friends helped themselves.

"Is today her birthday too?" John asked.

"Yes," I replied. "Impossible as it may seem, Scarlet and I were born on the very same day."

Scarlet got a key chain, a purse, a sparkly hair clip, some makeup, and lots of jewelry — not that I was looking or cared. Kelsey Tan, Scarlet's second-best friend — she had so many best friends she had to rank them First, Second, Third, and so on — gave her a pink T-shirt with the word *STAR* on the front. Scarlet's first-best friend, Zoe Carter, presented her own gift with a flourish.

Scarlet opened it and pulled out an iPod. At first she looked confused. She probably already had an iPod.

"I've been looking all over for this," she said. "Isn't this my iPod?"

"I stole it from you yesterday," Zoe said. "I filled it up with five hundred of my favorite songs and put it in this cute alligator case for you. Do you love it?"

"Thanks, Zo." Scarlet threw her arms around Zoe and they jumped up and down, screaming. They did that a lot.

Out of all that junk, the only decent present she got, I thought, was from Charlie Scott. He gave her a bouquet of blue flowers. Scarlet sniffed them. I could see by her face that they smelled really good.

Mr. Brummel passed through the hall just then, kicking through the tumbleweeds of crumpled wrapping paper on the floor. "Well, well — looks like we've got a birthday here?" he said.

"Two birthdays," Maybelle chimed in, nodding at me.

"Want a cupcake, Mr. B.?" Scarlet held out the white bakery box to him.

"No thanks." Mr. Brummel patted his stomach. "Watching my figure. Happy birthday, girls."

Scarlet unwrapped yet another tube of lip gloss and accidentally dropped it on the floor. The tube rolled across the hall, bumping my foot. I picked it up.

"I'll get it," Zoe said. She crossed the hall and held out her hand.

"Today is Schmitzy's birthday too," Maybelle told her.

"Like I care," Zoe said. "Hand it over."

I gave her the lip gloss. As if I wanted the stupid thing.

Zoe ran back across the hall. "You might want to take this back to the store," she said, handing the gloss to Scarlet. "It's all gross now. It's been in the *Lav.*"

They laughed. Scarlet dropped the gloss into her bag.

I wasn't trying to catch her eye — I went out of my way to avoid that kind of attention — but I did, by mistake. She had a strange expression on her face — not sad, exactly, but confused, like something was wrong. But what could possibly go wrong for the prettiest, most popular girl in the school? Especially on her birthday, which looked pretty great from where I was standing.

She looked away quickly and went back to laughing with her friends. I figured I'd imagined the whole thing. Something made me glance down the hall to see if Mr. Brummel had witnessed my latest humiliation. He was just disappearing around the corner. So he probably hadn't.

There was a time when a mean comment like Zoe's would have crushed me. I used to get crushed on a daily basis. I'd been called Yeti, Hairball, Furby. . . . The worst was when someone started a rumor that I was so hairy I needed to go to a dog groomer. That one really got to me for some reason.

But by the time I turned thirteen I was tough. No one could hurt me. I'd heard every insult anyone could sling at me. Or at least I thought I had.

The bell rang for first period. Scarlet hugged her thousands of friends. They all sang "Happy Birthday" to her as they walked to class.

"*That's* what a birthday is supposed to be like," I said.

"Don't worry, Schmitzy," Maybelle said. "It's only nine o'clock in the morning. There's lots of time left for birthday surprises."

"Oh, I know," I said, feeling lower than ever.

Maybelle was right — there were plenty of birthday surprises left to come that day.

In the cafeteria, Zoe "accidentally" splattered my shirt with beefaroni when I was in line behind her.

"I'm so sorry, Lav," Zoe said. "But don't worry — you can't even see the stain. Your shirt's already dirty."

Next, Ms. Kantner caught me slipping a note to Maybelle in English. As punishment, she read it to the class out loud.

M— Do you think I need to start using deodorant? Sometimes after gym I feel like I have B.O. Do I stink right now? —L.

That got a big response from the whole class.

The only good part of the day came right after school. Mr. Brummel held a meeting for everyone auditioning for the fall musical, *The Music Man*.

It was my dream to play Marian the Librarian in *The Music*

Man. I'd decided to audition even though I knew I'd never get the part — after the "Tiny Bubbles" disaster, I was sure nobody wanted to be on a stage with me anytime soon. But I couldn't resist a chance to sing "Goodnight, My Someone" in public just once, even if it was only for an audition.

The auditorium was packed with girls who wanted to be Marian. I knew I had a snowball's chance in Miami, but I had to try.

"I didn't expect such a big crowd," Mr. Brummel told us. "I think we'll have to divide the auditions into two afternoons. Everyone with a last name starting with *A* through *L* will audition tomorrow, and *M* through *Z* will go the next day."

Good, I thought. That gave me an extra day to practice.

"The theater is full of traditions and superstitions," Mr. Brummel went on. "And magic. An actor can transform into a whole new person right in front of your eyes. You've probably heard that it's good luck to say 'break a leg' before a performance. Well, back in my school days in Kalamazoo we had a different good luck rhyme we chanted before auditions."

Then he told us the rhyme:

Know the role you want to play
And say the name three times this way:
backward, forward,
upward, downward,
inward, outward,
eastward, westward,

northward, southward,

most of all, heavenward.

A few people snickered. Mr. Brummel got a little carried away with the "theater magic" sometimes.

But I needed a good luck charm. I vowed to try out Mr. Brummel's superstitious rhyme right before my audition.

And I did, sort of.

That's when everything went kablooey.

2

The Plastic Princess

I couldn't wait to turn thirteen. Everyone said it was an unlucky number, but I didn't care. I'd always been lucky. I had a nice house, nice clothes, a starting spot on the soccer team, the coolest friends . . . what more could I want?

So I was feeling good when I walked into the kitchen on the morning of my thirteenth birthday and found Ben, my fourteen-year-old stepbrother, eating Lucky Charms.

I opened the refrigerator and said good morning.

He looked up. I waited for him to wish me a happy birthday. Instead he bowed and said, "Your Plasticity," sweeping the floor with his arm. Then he stuffed more Lucky Charms into his mouth.

He usually called me The Plastic Princess. Variations included Your Plastitude, Princess Plasticide, and The Royal Pain.

It wasn't fair. There was nothing plastic about me. *He* was the one with a mouth full of plastic braces.

I took a deep yoga breath. I stayed positive, even in the face of extreme negativity.

Maybe he doesn't know it's my birthday, I thought. After all, we'd only been brother and sister for less than a year.

"Guess what," I said. "It's my birthday."

"What do you want, a plastic cake?" He didn't bother to look up from his cereal bowl. "To go with your plastic head?"

Very deep yoga breaths. "My head is not plastic," I said.

"My mistake," Ben said. "I meant polyvinyl chloride. Technical error."

I grabbed a yogurt and sat down at the table. I had a pile of presents waiting at my place. Normally I'd wait for my mom before opening them, but a lot of the time I left for school before she was done getting ready. So I started opening them. I found a red velvet jacket, a pair of silver tights, a flower pin for my hair, and some makeup. Exactly what I wanted.

"Why don't you get it over with and move into the mall for good?" Ben said. "You could start a new civilization with others of your kind: The Plastic People. Anthropologists will identify you by your empty eyes and your ugly silver tights."

"You're the one who's eating Lucky Charms," I sputtered. "They're practically made out of plastic." I knew it was a lame comeback. But deep yoga breaths were powerless against Ben.

Mom came in, still in her bathrobe, trailed by Steve in

his suit, ready for work. Steve was my new stepfather. His head was like a big square block. Mom said he seemed gruff on the outside, but if I gave him a chance I'd see how nice he could be. Mom and I used to live in a townhouse in Cross Keys, but after the wedding we moved to a mansion on Goodwood Gardens. I would have liked our new house — if it hadn't come with a stepbrother and a stepfather.

"Happy Birthday, sweetie!" Mom had some kind of green cream all over her face. It got on my sweater when she kissed me. "How do you like your presents?"

Steve held up the silver tights. "What the heck is this?"

"Fashion from outer space," Ben cracked.

Mom took the tights away from Steve and gave him a mug of coffee. "They're very stylish," she explained.

Steve shrugged and sipped his coffee. Mom turned to me and studied my head like it was a giant pimple that needed popping.

"I don't like that green eye shadow on you," she said. She picked through my pile of presents until she found the taupe eye shadow she'd bought me. "Try this. Less garish."

"Mom, I don't have time to change my makeup now," I said. "I'll be late. Besides, green is the cool color."

"All the Plastic People are wearing it," Ben said.

Mom pressed the taupe shadow into my hand. "You can fix it in the bathroom when you get to school. Ben, you can keep your opinions to yourself. The last thing my daughter needs is to follow your fashion advice." She looked disapprovingly at his jeans, which he'd worn for something like thirty days in a row.

"Whatever you say, Boss Lady." Ben saluted her and clicked his heels.

"Steve, what did I tell you about the way he talks to me?" Mom said.

"Ben, cool it," Steve said.

"I'm a rebel," Ben said. "You can't keep us rebels down."

A rebel. Please. "What are you rebelling against?" I asked.

He smiled. "Anything you throw my way."

It was a big house, but somehow when we were all in the same place it felt tiny.

I felt better once I got to school. I loved school. I knew how to work it. School was my world.

I turned down the eighth-grade hall. Zoe and Kelsey were whispering to each other. When she saw me, Zoe stopped talking and flashed me a big smile. They'd been doing a lot of whispering lately. Probably planning a big birthday surprise for me.

Zoe ran up to me and shouted, "Happy Birthday! Happy Birthday! You're finally one of us!" She gave me a big hug and we jumped up and down and screamed, "Teenagers! Teenagers!"

A small crowd waited for me at my locker. The whole posse, and even a few boys, like Ian Colburn, who Zoe liked, and Charlie Scott.

I kind of had a crush on Charlie. Zoe said he was beneath me. NOK: Not Our Kind. But I really REALLY liked him. What got me was the way he hid behind his hair. He was shy. But if you said the right thing to him, he came out and gave you this big smile. It didn't happen that often, but it happened. It was like the sun coming out from behind a cloud.

Charlie gave me a bunch of flowers. Bright blue carnations. I sniffed them. They had no smell. But they were the most beautiful flowers I'd ever seen.

"Carnations," Zoe whispered to me. "So *cheap*. They sell them at the gas station!"

I didn't care. Charlie had remembered my birthday.

"What's everybody doing this afternoon?" Zoe asked. "Want to come over to my house and hang out for a while?" She aimed this right at Ian.

"Can't," Ian said. "Soccer practice."

I had soccer practice too. "What about after practice," I said. "What are you doing, Charlie?"

"I'm trying out for the musical," Charlie replied. "There's a big meeting about the auditions after school today."

The musical. Charlie was so talented he was sure to get a part. If Charlie played the boy lead and I played the girl lead, I'd get to kiss him in rehearsal every day for weeks. Just about the only thing I knew about musicals was that people were always kissing in them.

I decided then and there. "I'm going to try out too," I said.

"Scarlet, to be in a musical you have to *sing*," Kelsey said.

"I know that," I said.

"I'm just trying to be helpful." Kelsey pushed a present into my hand. "Here, open mine."

I got so many presents I was swimming in wrapping paper. Zoe saved hers for last. She'd filled my iPod with songs I didn't know and got me a new alligator case.

"Thanks, Zo," I said. My taste in music was kind of grandma — Zoe always teased me about it, so she liked to give me new songs.

I heard a snort and glanced across the hall. Lavender Schmitz and her friend Maybelle and this guy John Obrycki were watching us.

Lavender and I had the same birthday. It kind of challenged my belief in astrology. No two people could've been more different than me and Lavender.

"Looks like Lavender hasn't been to the dog groomer for a while," Zoe whispered. "Wonder when her next appointment is? She could really use a trim."

"Maybe she can get the groomer to put one of those little puff balls on top of her head," Kelsey added. "Like poodles have?"

"You guys . . ." I said. The dog groomer joke was getting old.

I watched Lavender and her friends for a second while I listened to my iPod. John Obrycki made a star out of paper and gave it to Lavender. The star was so pretty. It must be like magic, I thought, to be able to make something out of nothing that way.

A tiny voice in my head said, *Lavender is lucky.*

What a strange thing to think. I was sure I didn't mean it. *I* was lucky. Lavender wasn't lucky at all. She was just about the unluckiest person I knew.

Before soccer practice I went to the auditorium for the musical meeting. I wasn't sure what drew me there, really. It wasn't only the chance to kiss Charlie, or even all the attention I'd get if I scored a lead role. It was something else, something stronger, but mysterious.

Mr. Brummel talked about the magic of the theater. He taught us this rhyme to say when you wanted a part with all your heart — like a spell you could cast. He said that when you're onstage you get to be someone else. Like a vacation from yourself.

Maybe that was what attracted me to the play. I liked being myself, but sometimes I was curious to see what it would be like to have a different life. A princess, or a movie star, or . . . anyone.

Little did I know, I was about to find out.

3

A Girl Who Carries a Purse

"Happy birthday, Lavender Blue," my mother sang at the Special Birthday Dinner in the kitchen that night. She kissed me on the cheek.

She named me Lavender and my sister Rosemary after an old song based on a nursery rhyme, "Lavender Blue and Rosemary Green." I wished she'd made my middle name Blue instead of Myrtle.

"Thirteen years old," Dad said. "Yeesh. Do you wear a bra yet?"

Rosemary laughed.

For the record, I had a bra but I didn't really need one. I only wore it on special occasions. So far, an occasion special enough hadn't come up.

"Frank, you don't ask a young lady questions like that," Mom said.

"Even if she's your daughter?" Dad said. "Even if you changed her diapers hundreds of times?"

"I'm sorry you had to change my diapers, Dad, okay?" I said. "Can you let it go? Am I going to have to hear about diapers for the rest of my life?"

"When you have kids of your own you can tease them as

much as you want," Dad said. "Take out your frustration with me on them. That's how it works."

"*Frank*," Mom scolded. "Don't listen to him, Lavender." She picked up a strand of my hair, then let it drop and wiped her hand on her jeans, as if she'd just touched toxic slime. "Oh, Lav, aren't you going to wash your hair today? It's your birthday."

"I know it's my birthday," I said. "That means I get to do what I want. And I don't want to wash my hair."

"But it's so *dirty*." Mom wouldn't let it go. "You have to pay attention to these things now that you're growing up."

I liked being clean as much as anybody. I just didn't always feel like washing my hair. I had better things to do. Like sing along with my records. Or stare into space. And what difference did it make, anyway? Nobody noticed me, except to be mean to me. If I had clean hair, would everybody suddenly start throwing rose petals in my path?

I didn't think so.

"Anyway," I said, "it's just us here in the kitchen. What do you care if my hair is clean or not?"

"I care," Rosemary said. "I lose my appetite looking at your icky hair."

"Oh dear, we wouldn't want that, would we?" Rosemary was ten and in no danger of starving to death.

"Rosemary will lose her baby fat when she gets her growth spurt," Mom said. That's what she always said. I was still waiting for *my* famous growth spurt.

Rosemary was like a littler, blonder version of me. Her

glasses made her watery blue eyes look huge. She was always sniffling, a habit even I had been spared.

"Time for presents!" Dad said, changing the subject. He was a big fan of subject-changing.

First came Rosemary's present. She always gave me something she'd made at school. I opened it.

An ashtray.

Why did Rosemary's art teacher keep teaching kids how to make ashtrays? I didn't smoke. Nobody in my family smoked. But Rosemary brought home enough ashtrays to furnish a tobacco shop.

"It's a ukulele pick holder," Rosemary explained.

"Thank you, Rosemary," I said. I appreciated her explanation — it was the most creative part of the gift.

"Now open ours." Dad set a square box in front of me, nicely wrapped. It could've been anything — anything *except* what I'd asked for, which was the complete boxed set of the late, great Hawaiian music master Don Ho's classic LP records. This box was too small for records, and too light.

I opened the present. Inside was a brown leather purse with a long shoulder strap and lots of buckles.

I looked at Mom and Dad. They were staring at me with wide eyes. Expecting me to love it.

Mom's eyes narrowed a bit. "Do you like it? It's from that store Maroc, on Thirty-Sixth Street. I asked around and found out all the girls shop there."

This was news to me. I wasn't much of a shopper.

"We picked it out together," Dad said.

"It's — it's —" I said.

Dad gave up and reached for another hamburger. "She hates it. Why do we even bother? She doesn't appreciate anything we do for her."

"That's not true," I said. "I just don't understand why you would buy this for me. I told you what I wanted. The complete boxed set of Don Ho. They have it at Lionel's Vinyl, and it probably costs a lot less than this purse." Lionel's Vinyl was a record shop in my neighborhood. I'd found an old record player in the attic — it used to belong to my dad — and went into Lionel's to buy records to play on it. I liked their scratchy sound.

"The price isn't the point," Mom said. "We wanted to get you something to show that we realize you're growing up. A young lady's present."

"But I'm not a young lady," I protested. "And I don't want to be."

Dad dropped his hamburger. "You're going to be whether you like it or not," he said. "You think I want to be a fat middle-aged man? No. But did anyone ask me? No. It's not up to me."

"Fine," I said. "But why do I have to be a young lady who carries a purse? Why can't I be a young lady who listens to Don Ho?"

"I didn't want to get you more records," Mom said. "You have too many already. And you spend too much time alone in your room. You need to get out more. Go to parties. See your friends. And when you go out, you'll need a purse."

This was great. My mother wanted me to get out of my room and go to parties.

"If you wanted me to be so social, why did you name me Lavender Schmitz?" I said. "Do you think 'Lav' is a girl who goes to parties carrying a purse?"

"I don't see what that has to do with anything," Mom said.

"How can you not see?" I cried. "I'm not asking for much. I'm not asking for a cute popular-girl name like Summer or Isabella. What's wrong with Jane? Or Kate? Or Sarah? Anything but Lavender!"

Mom looked like she was about to cry. I felt bad. Really bad. But I couldn't stop myself. It was as if my mouth had a personality of its own, completely independent from the rest of me, which, deep down, didn't want to hurt anyone.

"Maybe if you were nicer to people, you'd have more friends," Rosemary said.

"How would you know?" I snapped at her.

Dad slapped the table. "Can we get some cake here or what?"

The cake was a store-bought devil's food with pink frosting and an orange wax candle shaped like the number thirteen. I loved devil's food but the candle was really ugly.

Dad got up and lit the candle. "I tried to get a lavender candle," Mom said quietly. "Or even blue. But orange was all they had. Because Halloween's coming up, I guess."

They sang "Happy Birthday" and set the glowing cake in front of me. I felt like dropping my whole head on top of the cake and smashing it. But that only would have made things worse.

"Make a wish," Mom said.

I wish I were a totally different person, I thought. I remembered what Mr. Brummel had said that day, about how an actor could transform herself like magic. And for some reason Scarlet Martinez popped into my mind.

Scarlet backward was *Telracs*.

Telracs Telracs Telracs.

Scarlet Scarlet Scarlet.

The words came to me by themselves, swirling around the image of Scarlet. . . . Scarlet laughing, surrounded by friends and presents, so graceful and so happy . . .

"Hurry up and wish, Lav," Rosemary said. "The candle is melting all over the cake."

I wish I were a totally different person. With a totally different life.

And I blew out the candle.

4

The Big One-Three

When I got home from school, the house was dark and empty. I started turning on the lights. Where was everybody? Maybe they were planning a surprise party for me. The doorbell would ring and all my friends would pour in, or I'd walk into the den and everybody would jump out and yell "Surprise!"

When I turned six, and Mom was still married to Dad, my real dad, they surprised me with a tea party for all my favorite dolls and stuffed animals. Zoe was there too. Mom and Dad sat down with me and Zoe and our dolls and we ate cake and drank ginger ale out of the tea set they gave me.

I was remembering that long-ago birthday while I walked from room to room, turning on the lights. I knew that when Steve got home he'd complain that I was wasting electricity, but I didn't care. It was my birthday and I didn't want to be all alone in a dark house.

I took a vase off the coffee table and filled it with water for Charlie's flowers. I heard the car pull into the driveway. Mom and Steve were home from their tennis match.

"It's the birthday girl!" Mom kissed me, smearing red lipstick all over my cheek.

"Who turned on all the lights?" Steve asked. He didn't wait for an answer, just went from room to room flicking them off, except for the kitchen, where Mom and I were sitting on stools.

"I'm hungry," I said. "What are we having for dinner? Fettuccine Alfredo?" I loved fettuccine Alfredo, but Mom said it was so fattening we could only have it once a year, on my birthday.

"You can have anything you want," Mom said. "We're going out to dinner for your birthday."

"We are? Where?"

"The Charter House," Steve said. "One of my clients has just invested in it." Steve did some kind of work that involved clients and money. "It's a special occasion place — and this is a special occasion."

"You like the Charter House, don't you, Scarlet?" Mom asked.

I liked it okay. It was super fancy and super . . . stiff. The last time we'd gone there was after Steve's uncle's funeral.

"I don't mind," I said.

It wasn't like I had a choice.

I didn't need to worry about anyone singing "Happy Birthday" to me at the Charter House. It wasn't a singing

26

kind of place. It was very hushed and fancy. Everything gleamed: the candles and the silver, the buttons on the jackets of the waiters and the wine stewards. They didn't have fettuccine Alfredo on the menu, so I ordered lobster. Lobster was good too.

"Look at these prices," Steve said. "This place is practically a license to print money."

"Money, money, money . . ." Ben muttered.

Mom held the menu close to her face, then far away, staring at it. She'd been having trouble reading in dim light, I'd noticed.

"I'll read it to you if you want, Mom," I offered. I had perfect eyesight. Actually, better than perfect. Mom always said we were lucky we didn't need glasses.

Steve put his arm over Mom's shoulders. "Don't you think it's time to get some reading glasses?"

Mom sat back in her chair and stretched herself tall. "Are you saying I'm old?"

"No! I didn't say anything about anyone being old," Steve said. "I'm just trying to be practical. Besides, I bet you'll look great in glasses."

Mom glared at the menu. "I can read just fine without them." Then she stood up. "Excuse me. I'll be right back." She went to the ladies' room. She was big on going to the ladies' room.

Steve shook his head. "Your mother's too sensitive. Did I say she was old? Did I?"

Ben turned to me. "What about you, Princess P.? Going to get all touchy now that you're the big One-Three?"

"I'm not touchy." He annoyed me, but that didn't mean I was *touchy*.

"Go easy on her, Ben," Steve said. "Girls her age start to go a little nutsy."

When Mom came back from the bathroom, she had more lipstick on and her hair was poofed up higher. The waiter brought our entrées. He cracked open my lobster for me so I wouldn't get all messy.

"What's your week look like, Ben?" Steve asked.

"*Skullmuncher 7* comes out Friday," Ben said. "Vartek and I are going straight from school to stand in line for it at GameMaster."

Vartek was the loser Ben had somehow convinced to be his friend. "What's *Skullmuncher 7*?" I asked.

"It's only the greatest game in human history," Ben said.

"Those game companies make a fortune," Steve said.

"I don't care about that, Dad," Ben said. "I like *Skullmuncher* because it's sick."

"It certainly sounds sick." Mom frowned in disapproval.

"*Sick* means *good*," Ben explained.

"I knew that," Mom said. She totally did not.

"Ben, don't look down your nose at money," Steve said. "If I didn't work hard to earn money, you wouldn't be able to afford to buy your games."

Ben's mouth flapped open, and then, for once, he shut it without making a sound. Ha.

"What about you, Scarlet?" Mom asked. "What are your plans this week?"

"I have a big soccer game tomorrow," I said. "And I'm going to try out for the musical."

"The musical!" Mom said. "That's nice, honey. We did *Guys and Dolls* in high school. I played a gangster's moll."

"Mr. Brummel told us about this old superstition that's supposed to help you when you audition," I said. "You say the name of the part you want three times, in all these different ways. Did you ever hear of that, Mom?"

"Not that I remember," Mom said.

"What do you mean, all these different ways?" Ben said.

"Backward, forward, upward, downward, inward, outward, eastward, westward, northward, southward, and most of all, heavenward," I recited.

"Like in *The Shining*, when the little kid keeps saying *redrum*, and it's 'murder' spelled backward?" Ben said. "Redrum! Redrum!"

"No," I said. "It's not like that at all."

Ben bunched up his napkin in his fist. "Musicals are so weak."

"I never was a big fan myself," Steve said. "Who breaks out in song in the middle of the street? It's not believable."

"In *Skullmuncher*, the only things that go *heavenward* are the bodies of all the zombies I waste," Ben said.

"I wasn't talking about *Skullmuncher*," I said. "*The Music Man* is a totally different thing."

"'*The Music Man*'?" Ben mocked me. "That's what it's called? That's the wussiest title I've ever heard. I can't believe your plastic friends are letting you try out for it."

"I didn't ask for your opinion," I said.

"Honey, Ben's trying to relate to you in his own way," Mom said. She was always trying to get me to *understand* him, to remember that his mother had moved to California and left him behind with Steve. She claimed that Ben missed his mother, even though he never said so and didn't show it. Hey, we all had problems. I missed my dad, but he was busy with his new wife and new baby. I also missed Mom, the way she used to be before she married Steve. I didn't believe Ben was sad, and even if he was, that was no excuse for picking on me.

The waiter brought out a plate of petit fours and a pink cake topped with a hideous orange candle shaped like the number thirteen. Just as I'd hoped, no one sang "Happy Birthday." It would have been embarrassing.

I looked around the table in the glow of my one birthday candle. Mom smiled proudly. Steve signaled the waiter for the check. Ben was kicking his chair. The waiter put Mom's leftover steak on the table, wrapped in foil shaped like a swan.

The foil swan made me think of origami, and John Obrycki's star.

I didn't really make a wish. But when I closed my eyes and blew out the candle, I saw that paper star, and Lavender Schmitz's face.

Which was strange. Lavender Schmitz's face was not something I normally thought about. At all.

Nothing special happened after that. We went home. I went to bed.

I lay in the dark and thought about Charlie. The Anti-Ben. He'd never call *The Music Man* wussy. I would've bet he didn't spend all his time playing *Skullmuncher* either.

I imagined starring in the musical with Charlie. Gazing into his eyes as we sang a duet. Holding hands as we took our bows at the final curtain. Sneaking a kiss backstage.

I really, really, really wanted to play Marian. But I'd never sung alone in front of people before. Not in a serious way, like onstage. I needed all the luck I could get.

I decided to test out Mr. Brummel's superstition. It probably wouldn't work, but what was the harm in trying?

I got out of bed. I said *Nairam Nairam Nairam* three times.

Then I said *Marian Marian Marian* three times forward.

I said it looking up.

I said it looking down.

I said it breathing in.

I said it breathing out.

I said it facing east, west, north, and south.

I clapped my hands together in prayer and chanted the name to the heavens. *Marian Marian Marian.*

Then I climbed back into bed and fell asleep. In my pretty room with the frilly bedspread, the pink canopy, and the striped wallpaper I'd picked out myself. And Charlie's flowers in a vase on my dresser.

5

Pink Purgatory

I knew something was wrong the minute I woke up. Everything around me was pink.

Pink sheets, pink frilly canopy over the bed, pink-striped wallpaper . . . everything was so pink I thought I was looking at the inside of my eyelids. Or else having a very bad dream.

I blinked. The pink was still there.

What day is it? I wondered. The last thing I remembered was Mom saying, "I hope you had a happy birthday, Lavender," and kissing me good night. And Dad saying, "Maybe next year will be better. Don't give me that look — it could happen."

Then I fell asleep in my room, which was not pink. Not pink at all.

So how did I end up here, surrounded by pink?

I sat up and bumped my knee against my head. Ow! That had never happened before. My legs seemed awfully long all of a sudden. And bare. Hadn't I been wearing my flannel cowboy pajamas when I went to bed?

I stood up and knocked my head. Maybe my fabled growth spurt had come at last! Along with some kind of weird pink vision problem.

I'd knocked my head against a stupid frilly canopy thing. Across the room I saw a life-size poster of a girl who looked just like Scarlet Martinez. Now I knew for sure this was a nightmare.

I stepped toward the wall for a better look. That girl didn't just look like Scarlet. She *was* Scarlet!

I twitched. The Scarlet poster seemed to move.

I raised my arm. The Scarlet poster raised her arm too.

This was no poster.

This was a mirror!

I turned my head left and right. In the mirror, Scarlet copied my movements exactly.

I was looking at myself. And that self looked just like Scarlet.

I felt like screaming. But I was afraid to breathe.

My mind raced. Was I possessed? Was this some kind of Alice in Wonderland Through the Looking Glass situation? Or . . . I know . . . a reality TV show!

Someone knocked on my door. Maybe this was the camera crew.

"Scarlet, are you up yet, sweetie?" a woman's voice called.

I froze. *What should I do?*

Another knock. "Scarlet?"

Definitely not my mother's voice.

I looked down at my storky legs. Scarlet's legs. Such knobby knees. I grabbed a terry cloth bathrobe and threw it over the tank top and boy shorts Scarlet's body had slept in.

Knock knock knock. "Scarlet! Time to get up." The door opened. In walked a deeply tanned, deeply blond woman wearing a tennis skirt and carrying a racket. She looked a lot like Scarlet.

"It's the day after your birthday! Do you feel different now that you're thirteen?"

Did I feel different? What kind of question was that? I couldn't have felt more different if I'd woken up in a bird's nest. I was a different species. I moved my mouth, but no words came out. My tongue flapped uselessly against the roof of my mouth, as if I couldn't remember how to work it.

"Does your throat hurt?" Scarlet's mother asked.

"I feel different," I said. My voice was weirdly high and squeaky. Scarlet's voice. "Yes, I feel totally different."

"Get up, Scarlet!" a man's voice shouted from the hall. "Birthday's over."

"Did you thank Steve for dinner last night?" Scarlet's mother asked. "You know how he likes to feel appreciated —"

Steve? Who was Steve?

This was all very confusing. I had to sit down.

Scarlet's mother sat beside me and put her arm around me. "Are you feeling all right? Something looks different about you. Around the eyes —" She stared at me. "I don't think I've seen that expression for a long time. You look . . . confused. And worried. Did you have a bad dream?"

Confused and worried? *Confused and worried?* That was putting it mildly. I wanted to get out of there and clear my head. "I'd better get to school," I squeaked. At least at school I knew who was who and where I was.

"Have some breakfast first," Scarlet's mother said. "And say good morning to Ben and Steve."

"Who are Ben and Steve?" I asked.

"Don't be smart," Scarlet's mother snapped. "Get dressed and come downstairs soon, before Steve leaves for work. Hurry up."

She left, shutting the door behind her. I opened Scarlet's closet. It was crammed with clothes. What should I wear? There was too much to choose from, all of it so girly I could puke.

I threw on a pair of jeans and a T-shirt. One look at myself in the mirror and I realized maybe I should put a bra on under it. So I rifled through the top drawer — so much frilly stuff, *ick* — and picked out the least frilly thing I could find, a sports bra.

I glanced in the mirror again. It was hard not to — there were mirrors on every wall. Even in just a T-shirt and jeans, I looked . . . well, pretty. Very pretty. It was scary how easy it was.

Socks and sneakers, and I was dressed. My hair was already shockingly clean, so there was no need to deal with that. Scarlet had her own bathroom — very convenient. I splashed a little water on my perfect skin. . . .

Wait, what was that? A mole on my jaw with a fine blond hair curling out of it?

Guess nobody's perfect after all.

Close enough, though. I noticed a lot of cleansers and creams around the bathroom sink but I had no idea what to do with them, so I didn't bother.

I grabbed the book bag I found hanging off the doorknob, put on a jacket, and went downstairs. This was one fancy house. A big chandelier dangled over my head, and everything was pure white. I mean *white* white. In my house this white rug would have stayed clean for about two seconds before someone dropped a piece of toast with blackberry jam and ruined it forever.

Scarlet's mother stood at the sink drinking juice, while a man in a suit and a teenage boy munched pastries at the kitchen island.

"Scarlet, why are you dressed like that?" her mother asked. "Is there a volunteer project today?"

She was right — I hardly ever saw Scarlet in such plain clothes. "Um, I'm in a casual mood." I grabbed a cinnamon roll off a plate and took a bite.

"Hey!" the boy grunted, as if they were all for him.

"Scarlet?" Her mother looked surprised. I guessed Scarlet was not a big cinnamon roll fan.

"What?" I shrugged. "I'm hungry."

Scarlet's mother nodded at the man in the suit — I figured he was Steve — reminding me to say something to him. "Good morning, Steve," I said. "Thank you for dinner last night."

"My pleasure, Scarlet."

I turned to the boy. He had crumbs stuck in his braces. "Good morning . . . Ben?"

"Yes, that's B-E-N," the boy snarked. "What's wrong, the plastic seep into your brain?"

"What plastic?" I asked.

Ben shook his head and laughed. Whatever. None of this mattered to me. Ben and Steve, whoever they were, were

Scarlet's problem. I hoped I'd never have to lay eyes on them again.

"Okay, well, I'm going to school." I snatched another cinnamon roll and left.

It was time to find my body.

6

Bad Hair Life

The morning after my birthday, I woke up to a blur.

I rubbed my eyes. Still blurry.

I turned on the light but that didn't help. My hand hit something on the nightstand. A pair of glasses.

Why did I have glasses on my nightstand? I had perfect vision. I did not wear glasses.

I put them on, just to see what would happen.

My eyesight cleared up right away.

I guess this is a dream, I thought. But it felt so real.

That's when I looked down at my feet. And saw the toes.

There was *hair* on my *toes*.

I screamed. And screamed again.

And again.

I paused. Had I woken up from the nightmare yet?

I looked down at my feet.

Hair on my *toes*!

Then I realized, *Those aren't my toes.*

They were way too stubby. And the nails weren't Cotton Candy Pink. I'd painted them the night before my birthday — two coats.

But if they weren't my toes, then *whose toes were they? And what were they doing on my feet?*

These aren't my feet, I thought, sliding my hand over the thick ankles. Not my legs either.

And who had picked out these bulky flannel pajamas? I leaned down and peered at them through the glasses. Cowboys. The pajamas were decorated with little cowboys and lassos.

I'd woken up as some kind of flannel-wearing miniature Yeti.

The door burst open and a woman I didn't know ran in. Probably freaked out by the screaming.

"Honey! What's the matter? What's wrong?" the woman asked.

"Who are you?" I cried.

The woman sat down on the bed.

"Get away from me!" I shouted.

The woman reached out to stroke my hair. "Shhh . . . it's okay, Lavender. You're having a bad dream."

I knocked her hand away. I didn't want some stranger touching my hair. Then *I* touched my hair, and it felt funny.

Thick. Coarse. Greasy.

My hair actually felt *dirty*!

"What's wrong with my hair?" I shrieked.

"Lavender, honey, that's what happens when you don't wash it enough," the woman said.

I pressed myself against the headboard. This wasn't my beautiful bedroom. This room was much smaller.

And dark. And messy. Clothes — horrible clothes I would never wear in a million years — carpeted the floor.

"Everything is okay, Lavender," the woman said. "Want some breakfast? I made French toast and scrapple."

Scrapple? What was scrapple? And who was this strange, squat woman? Had Mom hired a new cleaning lady? Why did she keep calling me *Lavender*?

A mirror hung, crooked, on the wall across the room. I walked over to it and stared at my reflection.

Staring back at me was a short, dark-haired girl wearing glasses.

I straightened the mirror. This had to be some kind of trick.

The girl in the mirror wasn't me. She was Lavender Schmitz.

"Better get a move on, Lav," the woman said. "You'll be late for school." She left, closing the door behind her.

I sat down on the bed and touched my stubby little polish-free toes. This had to be a terrible dream. There was no way I could be Lavender Schmitz. Ever. In a million years.

I gave myself the hardest pinch I could stand. If this was a dream, I wanted to wake up NOW.

PINCH!

OW!

It didn't work. No matter how hard I pinched myself, I still had those stubby toes.

I was Lavender.

But how?

I thought back. Back to the day before. My thirteenth birthday.

Had something unusual happened? Had I committed some terrible crime?

What could I possibly have done that would be *this* bad?

And where was Lavender? Was she in my body? In my clothes? In my room?

I searched the room for something decent to wear, straightening things up as I went. It was hard enough to find something clean. I settled on a brown skirt and some flats. Ugh. That shade of brown did nothing for Lavender's complexion. But then, what would?

I crept out to the hall and down the stairs. I heard some noise in the kitchen — Lavender's family eating breakfast. No time to deal with them now, I decided. I had to get to school and find Lavender. I had to straighten this out, and fast. What if I got stuck this way?

I couldn't imagine anything worse.

7

Unexpectedly Popular

Must find Scarlet. Must find Scarlet.

"Hi, Scarlet!" people called to me as I walked down the eighth-grade hall.

"Uh, hi," I said.

It felt strange saying hi to so many people. They knew me but I didn't know them. I didn't even know some of their names. I'd never bothered to learn many people's names, since I rarely needed to use them. Some had seeped into my brain through osmosis.

I headed for my locker and spun the combination.

"Scarlet, what are you doing at Lavender's locker?" Kelsey Tan asked.

Shoot. I wasn't even sure which locker was Scarlet's. And I didn't know her combination. What was I supposed to do? I tried to think of what Scarlet would say.

I tossed my hair. "Oh, gosh, what an airhead I am! What am I doing here? I got lost for a second, even though I've been going to school here for two whole years. What's an empty-headed girlbot to do?"

Kelsey looked at me funny and reflexively reached for her

cell phone. Maybe she thought she should call the police, or a doctor. I couldn't blame her. My imitation of Scarlet was extremely unconvincing.

But then Kelsey laughed, as if I'd just told the funniest joke ever. "Come on," she said. "Let's go to our lockers."

"Okay," I said. "But first I really have to pee." What would Kelsey say when I stood stupidly at Scarlet's locker, unable to remember the combination? I hurried to the girls' bathroom to hide.

I walked in and checked the mirror. Still Scarlet.

"There you are!"

The voice — eerily familiar — came from a bathroom stall. I peeked under the door and saw two chunky legs — my good old legs! — and my one pair of "nice" shoes, the blue flats Mom had made me wear to my cousin's wedding.

The stall door burst open and out walked . . . me. It was really weird to look down at myself from above.

"Wow, I'm short," I said.

"You sure are," Scarlet snapped. "Now give me my body back!"

"Gladly," I said. "Tell me how."

"I don't know how! You tell me! What did you do, cast a spell on me or something, you —" She stopped, taking me in. "How could you dress me like that?"

"Like what?"

"You have to wear boots with those jeans or they look all wrong. And I work out in that T-shirt. It's not for school!"

"So?"

She stared at the side of my face and gasped. "The hair! You didn't pluck it!"

"I didn't *what*?"

"My mole hair! You went out in public, in my body, with a hair sticking out like that?" She grabbed at my face. I remembered the little blond hair sticking out of the mole on her jaw. Apparently she was going to rip it out with her bare hands. I backed off.

"Hey, watch it!" I pushed her away.

"You watch it!" She pushed back, and soon we were grabbing and clawing at each other like a couple of mud wrestlers.

The first period bell rang. I freed myself from her surprisingly strong grip, the little mole hair intact.

"Now what do we do?" Scarlet asked.

"I guess we'd better go to class," I said.

"But I want my body back!"

"So do I!" The second bell rang. I didn't know what to do.

"What time do you have lunch today?" Scarlet asked.

"Twelve-twenty-five," I said. "You?"

"Eleven-fifty," she said. "So we can't meet then."

"What about right after school?"

"Yes — we'll meet here as soon as classes are over," Scarlet said. "But in the meantime, *think*. Don't pay attention to your classes. Try to figure this out! And if you come up with any answers, find me right away."

"I will."

"And whatever you do, don't tell anybody about this!" Scarlet said.

"Don't worry," I said. "I'm not stupid."

I opened the bathroom door, then stopped. "Um, what class do I have?"

"French," Scarlet said. "What class do I have?"

"Algebra," I said.

"There isn't a quiz, is there?" Scarlet said.

"Actually, there is," I said.

"Great," Scarlet muttered. We quickly exchanged locker combinations and class schedules. Then we stormed out of the bathroom.

Off to French class. *This should be a treat*, I thought. I took Spanish.

I managed to fake my way through French, feigning a choking fit when Madame Geller called on me to read a dialogue with Charlie Scott. She sent me outside for a drink of water and I didn't come back until class was almost over. When she asked if I was okay, I answered, "*Oui, Madame.*"

Luckily she fell for it.

In gym we played basketball. People kept passing the ball to me as if they thought I could do something with it. The first time someone threw me the ball, I dropped it. The next time, I threw the ball right back. The third time, everyone was shouting, "Shoot! Shoot the ball!" So I aimed at the basket and threw. The ball ended up in the bleachers.

On to lunch. Always so delightful.

"Scarlet, over here!"

Zoe waved to me from across the cafeteria. I gulped and carried my lunch to her table. I'd been hoping to avoid this, but a girl's got to eat.

I sat down with Zoe, Kelsey, Marissa, and Saylor. "You looked a little shaky in gym this morning," Zoe said to me. "I hope you're not feeling off on game day."

"Game day?" I asked. "What are you talking about?"

"The big game?" Zoe said. "This afternoon? Against the Cheetahs?"

Big game? Big game of what?

I had a feeling she wasn't talking about Bananagrams.

Then I remembered the weird-looking shoes at the bottom of Scarlet's gym locker. Right. Scarlet played soccer.

I barely knew how to play. I could only hope my new body would take care of that for me, somehow. Scarlet's legs would know what to do without me. Wasn't there something called muscle memory?

"Wish me luck," I said.

Kelsey laughed. "Luck? You're the highest scorer on the team."

Uh-oh.

I tried to joke my way out of it. "Ha ha. Not for long."

"Quit kidding around," Zoe said. "This is a must-win game. The Cheetahs are undefeated. You have to be a superstar out there, Scar."

"We're going to whup those Cheetahs!" Kelsey cheered.

"The Cheetahs are toast!" Marissa said.

"Go Bees!" Saylor cried. Our team was called the Killer Bees. I knew that much. That, and that our mascot wore a bumblebee costume and a beehive hairdo.

Hand-stinging high fives all around.

"Well, don't forget," I said. "We're a team. Bees work together. I can't do it alone. Hooray for teamwork!"

Silence. My teamwork cheer fell flat.

"Woo! Go Scarlet!" Zoe said.

What would happen when they found out that an old lady with a sprained ankle could beat me at soccer? I had to find a way out of Scarlet's body, fast.

"Does anybody at this table know how to reverse a double-body metamorphosis?" I asked.

"What?" Zoe said.

"Never mind." I sighed.

It had been worth a shot.

8

Losing Sight of the Goal

The last bell rang. Finally, this horrible day was over.

Some of the low points:

Walking down the hall on the way to Lavender's Spanish class, I tripped over someone's foot and fell splat on my face. My books went flying. I hauled myself up and started picking up my books, but Zach Griffith — who I always thought of as one of my friends — snatched up my Spanish textbook and dangled it over my head. I reached for it — in my real body I could have grabbed it, but Lavender's body was too short. Zach laughed and tossed it to Adam Bender, who tossed it to Kieran Monahan, who'd had a crush on me since kindergarten and never would have teased me this way if he'd known it was *me*.

The bell rang. I was late for Spanish. "Give me the book!" I shouted, jumping up and down helplessly on my stubby little Lavender legs. But Kieran just tossed the book back to Zach, and around and around they went.

If only I could have said, "Kieran, it's me, Scarlet! The girl you've liked since you were five! I'll let you sit next to me in algebra if you'll just give back my Spanish book!"

But of course, if I'd said that, or anything like it, they would have only laughed harder.

When they finally had mercy and dropped the book, I grabbed it and hurried into Spanish class. "Lavender, *éstas tarde*," Señora Diaz said. I didn't know what that meant, but she was frowning, so I tried to find a seat. I spotted an empty one in the back row but when I went to sit down this girl I hardly even know put a book on the desk and said, "This seat's saved." So I tried the only other seat left, at the end of the second row. I wasn't dying to sit so close to the front, since I knew I was not going to understand anything that happened in class. But Señora Diaz was glowering at me more fiercely every second, so I took the second-row seat.

Jenna Friedberg was sitting at the next desk. "That seat's taken," she hissed.

"What do you mean? There's no one here," I whispered.

"It's *taken*," she repeated.

"I have to sit somewhere," I said.

"Sit somewhere else."

"Girls, let's settle down," Señora Diaz said in English, for which I was grateful.

I stayed in the seat next to Jenna, but she kept flicking tiny spitballs at me every time Señora Diaz turned her back. They were sticky and wet and really gross. I lifted my notebook cover as a shield, which helped a little. By the end of Spanish class, my notebook was plastered with tiny white spitballs.

In English class, Ms. Kantner asked Hallie Huff to pass out a story we were supposed to read. Hallie gave a copy to everyone in the class except for me. She walked right by me as if she didn't see me. I held up one hand in front of my face to make sure I was visible. There I was, stubby fingers and all, perfectly see-able.

"Hallie, you skipped me," I said. She didn't seem to hear me.

"Hallie, can I have a copy?" I asked. She ignored me.

"There's an extra copy," she told Ms. Kantner, and she went up to the front of the room and put the story on the teacher's desk. Of course there was an extra copy — she hadn't given me one.

"Thank you, Hallie," Ms. Kantner said.

I had to get up and walk to the front of the room. "I didn't get one, Ms. Kantner."

"Oh. Why didn't you say something to Hallie? Here you go, Lavender." She gave me the last copy.

I flashed Hallie an angry look as I walked back to my seat. She wrinkled her nose and looked away. Apparently I had become visible again.

Finally, after my last class, I stormed through the halls in search of Lavender. I was sure she'd swanned around school like a princess all day. Like she thought my life was one happy fairy tale. Well, compared to hers, it was. And I wanted it back.

"There you are!" Lavender stood in front of her locker — *my* locker — surrounded by boys — boys who had crushes on *me* — and Zoe and Kelsey. I grabbed her by the collar and tried to drag her into the bathroom where we could talk in private.

"What's your problem, Lav?" Kelsey said.

"Leave Scarlet alone," Zoe said. "Where are you taking her, your mother ship — *Lav*? Get it? The *lavatory* is her mother ship."

Zoe's "Lav" jokes were starting to seem less and less funny to me. One of the boys — Kieran — brushed me away. "I'll take care of this for you, Scarlet," he said to Lavender.

"Thanks," Lavender said. As if she were me! Which she so totally was not! Then she had the nerve to look down her — *my* — nose at me! I would have punched her right then if I hadn't been afraid of hurting my own face.

My whole day had been this way. People being mean to me for no reason. Ignoring me. Picking on me. Shunning me. Making fun of me. It was horrible. How did Lavender live like this?

The worst part was I could hardly blame people for being mean to me. I was on their side. I'd become such a klutz. Everything I did and said was embarrassing. I would have snubbed myself if I could.

"*Scarlet*," I said urgently. "We need to talk. About the *audition tomorrow*."

"Scarlet, come back," Kelsey said. "Don't waste your time with Dog-Breath."

An angry look flashed across Lavender's face — she was pissed. Even if Kelsey was kind of insulting me, she was really insulting Lavender. And Lavender didn't like it.

"Let's go outside," Lavender said.

We went out a side door and leaned against a brick wall.

"How did you do this to me?" I demanded. "I want you to reverse this spell right now!"

"How did *I* do it?" Lavender said. "I didn't do anything. Maybe *you* did it."

"Why would I do something like this to myself?" I asked. "Now switch us back and I promise not to tell anyone about it."

"Scarlet, I don't know how this happened," Lavender said. "I swear. I don't know how to switch us back."

I watched her face while she spoke, and I believed her. She didn't seem like a liar. Maybe she'd have been better off if she were.

We were in trouble.

"We've got to figure out how to fix this," I said. "Right away. Before I have to endure another moment as you. Do you know what I went through today?"

"Poor you," Lavender said. "Having to spend one whole day as me. Must be rough."

I guess I hadn't been as nice as I could have been. "I'm sorry. But come on, don't you want to go back to being yourself too?"

Before Lavender had a chance to answer, Zoe and Kelsey burst through the door and interrupted us. "Scarlet, let's go. You'll be late for the game."

Lavender looked at me.

"She'll be there in a minute," I said.

Kelsey rolled her eyes and walked away.

"Do I have to?" Lavender whined.

"Today's game is crucial," I told her. "If we beat the Cheetahs, we'll clinch a spot in the playoffs. Without me, they can't win. With you as me . . . I don't know. But I can't let down the team."

"Scarlet, come on!" Zoe shouted.

I looked down at my wide Lavender feet and stumpy Lavender legs. I'd been dropping things, spilling things, and bumbling around all day. Lavender's body was not built for soccer, that's all there was to it. And anyway, she wasn't on the team. I couldn't just insert myself into the game.

"You'd better go," I said. "We'll try to fix our problem right after the game. But don't mess up!" Lavender looked so uncertain that I added, "What do you know about soccer?"

"I know you try to kick the ball into the goal," Lavender said.

"That's it? That's all you know?"

She shrugged. "What do you want me to say?"

She was going to ruin my life. "Look," I said. "You're a forward. On the right side. People will pass you the ball. You kick it into the goal. Try not to let the other team get it. Okay? That's as simple as I can make it in the fifteen minutes we have before the game starts."

"I'll do my best," Lavender said. "Maybe your body will take over for me. I noticed it does that sometimes."

"I noticed that too. And it hasn't been a good thing. Don't botch it, Lavender. And whatever you do, don't touch the ball with your hands. Okay?"

"Okay."

"And if it comes near your head —"

"I know," she said. "Duck."

"No! Don't duck!" I smacked my face with my palm. "Head it! Bump the ball with your head."

"Seriously?"

"Yes, seriously!" Ack!

"Okay. I'll hit the ball with my head," Lavender said, but I could tell she wouldn't.

"I'll come watch the game and see how you do. Is there anything else I should know while I'm trapped inside your body?"

"There's a lot of stuff. I can't think of just one thing."

"All right. Go! You're going to be late." I pushed her toward the gym.

"Should I wear those spiky shoes in your locker?" she asked.

"Cleats," I said. "Yes. Wear them. My uniform is on the top shelf."

This was going to be a disaster.

It was weird watching myself play soccer. I sat in the stands with the crowd. There was my body (my good old body), out on the field in my black-and-yellow-striped uniform, Number 9. Lavender waved to me. Zoe said something to her. I could just imagine what. Probably "Why are you waving to that loser?"

Lavender had no idea how to warm up, but she was smart enough to look at the other girls and copy them.

Then the game started, and I wanted to die.

Lavender didn't know where to stand on the field. She was called off-sides on the first play. When the game finally started, she ran in the wrong direction.

Watching the game felt like one of those nightmares where someone is chasing you and you're trying to run away but you can't make your legs move. From the stands, I concentrated on my body, trying to will it to play well by remote control. All I did was give myself a headache.

Coach Kamen looked mystified. The crowd booed. Lavender kicked the ball out of bounds. She tripped over her feet when she dribbled the ball. When she tried to pass, the ball was intercepted by a girl on the other team, who quickly scored a goal. That happened three times.

She reeked.

We lost, 4–0. Coach Kamen pulled Lavender aside and stared into her eyes, looking for a sign of some problem. Was she sick? Losing her eyesight? Had she gone crazy? There was no other way to explain how a great player like me could suddenly be so lousy.

Then Zoe and Kelsey set in on her like two yapping Chihuahuas whose tails had been stepped on. I couldn't hear what they were saying, but they didn't look happy. I didn't mind missing the yelling. But then, if I'd played, we would have won, and they would have been carrying me off the field in triumph.

I saw Ben in the stands with his friend Vartek. It made it much worse to know he'd seen what had just happened. And to think that Lavender would soon be under my roof with him and the rest of my family.

Ben tapped Lavender on the shoulder, probably getting ready to say something dark and cruel. She turned and stared at him as if she wasn't quite sure who he was. I ran over and inserted myself between them.

"Hi, Scarlet," I said to Lavender. "Thanks for inviting me over to spend the night tonight." *Wink wink.*

"Who's this gargoyle?" Ben asked, pointing at me.

"This is my friend Lavender," Lavender said. "And she's not a gargoyle. She's the cutest girl in the school."

Ben snorted. "Yeah, right. Well, she can't come over tonight, Plastic P. The 'rents are having company, remember? And you're supposed to help get ready."

The Mortensons. I'd forgotten they were coming over. Mom always made me pass out hors d'oeuvres and drinks at her parties. She called it *hostess training.*

"What?" Lavender said. "I can't do that."

"Well, you have to," Ben said.

"Um, Scarlet and I have something important to do first," I said. "At my house."

We'd have to go to Lavender's house instead. We'd never get anything done at my house if Mom was having a dinner party.

"I don't care what you do," Ben said. "All I know is, the Mortensons are supposed to come over at seven thirty, and if you're not there, the Boss Lady is going to lose it."

"Don't worry, she'll be there," I said.

Ben drove off, north toward our house. Lavender and I walked in the other direction. She lived in Hampden. We passed big fancy houses, then smaller, shabbier houses, then brick row houses. As we crossed Keswick Road, a bird pooped on my head. That pretty much summed up my day.

"This is it." Lavender turned onto West 34th Street, a funky block of row houses decorated with pumpkins and witches and ghosts for Halloween.

I'd been in such a hurry to leave that morning I hadn't realized where I was. "Hey," I said. "Isn't this the Christmas Street?"

Lavender nodded. "We're the Crab House."

Lavender's block was famous. Every December all the neighbors decorated *insanely* for Christmas. Lights covered every inch of every house and yard. At night people lined up to see the spectacle, cars and people clogging the street as they slowed down to look. They showed it on the local news. It was a big deal. When I was little, my dad had taken me to see the Christmas Street every year. I hadn't been back since he'd gone.

There were mechanical Santas and reindeer flying across the street on wires, a giant tree made out of hubcaps and topped with a plastic dinosaur instead of a star, snowmen made from bike wheels painted white, a nativity scene populated entirely by teddy bears, and three toy trains that chugged from yard to yard on crazy winding tracks. One house had a Baltimore Ravens theme, the porch and yard filled with inflatable football players in purple and black Ravens uniforms.

And then there was the Crab House, featuring a giant blow-up crab in a Santa suit in a sleigh pulled by eight smaller crab-deer. The tree was decorated with empty cans of Old Bay spice and National Bohemian beer. It was hideous, but it had always been my favorite house: The Crab House people gave away free hot chocolate and cookies from their front porch.

"You really live in the Crab House?" I asked.

"Don't judge," Lavender said. "It gets my dad through the holidays."

We walked up the steps to Lavender's front porch, which was decorated with Indian corn for Halloween. I took a closer look at the scarecrow by the door. It had a crab head and red crab claws for hands.

Lavender shrugged. "He's really into crabs."

Christmas was less than two months away. What if I was still trapped in Lavender's body by then? Would I spend the holidays on the Christmas Street — with Lavender's family? In the Crab House?

No. No way. That could not happen.

We went inside. I smelled like bird poop. Nobody seemed particularly surprised.

9

The Candles of Kalamazoo

When Scarlet and I got home, Mom and Rosemary were in the kitchen having their afternoon snack while watching *Judge Judy*.

"Lavender!" Mom hugged Scarlet. I wished she'd hug me too. Just for old times' sake. "How was school today?"

"Okay," Scarlet said. "I'll be right back. I've got to wash my head."

"Oh, Lavender, not again." Mom turned Scarlet's head this way and that until she spotted the bird poop she hadn't managed to wipe off. "Do you need some help?"

"I'll help her," I offered. I was glad not to be the one with bird poop on her head for once.

"Who's this?" Mom stared right at me, her own daughter, as if I were a stranger.

"This is my friend Scarlet," Scarlet said.

"How nice!" Mom exclaimed. "It's *wonderful* to meet you, Scarlet. What a treat!" She was clearly thrilled that "I" had such a normal-looking — or yeah, okay, great-looking — friend all of a sudden. She probably thought I was going through a lot of big changes and getting all mature and undorkifying. I hated to disappoint her, but when Scarlet and I finally switched back I planned to go right back to my old self. Mom was just going to have to accept it.

"I've heard you make a killer grilled cheese sandwich," I said, hoping it would inspire her to make us some.

Mom practically batted her eyelashes at me. "I had no idea Lavender ever said anything nice about me. But she does love those grilled cheese sandwiches. Would you girls like some?"

"Thanks," Scarlet said. "We'll be upstairs in my room."

"Plotting and scheming," I added.

"All right," Mom said. "I'll bring up the sandwiches when they're ready."

Wow — even room service. She really wanted to impress my new friend.

Rosemary sat at the kitchen table the whole time, blinking at us from behind her big glasses. She looked from me to Scarlet and blinked faster than usual. She sensed something was wrong, I could tell. She knew perfectly well that I would never be friends with a girl like Scarlet.

"Hi, Rosemary," I said.

"How did you know my name?" She squinted at me suspiciously. "Lavender didn't introduce us."

"I told her all about you," Scarlet said.

Rosemary knew this was fishy. "You did?"

"Not *all* about you," I said. "She just warned me that her little sister Rosemary was a pest. So I'd know to avoid you when I got here."

Rosemary blinked again. I'd just said a very Lavender thing, and Rosemary knew it.

"We'd better get upstairs," I said to Scarlet. "Or that bird poop will dry into your hair permanently."

"Ohh!" Scarlet wailed. We ran upstairs, back to my good old room. Scarlet's room was fancy, but this was home.

Or at least it used to be home. When I got to my room I found that Scarlet had made my bed and picked up all my books, records, and dirty clothes off the floor. I saw my rag rug for the first time in months. I'd almost forgotten I *had* a rug.

"Hey." I hardly recognized the place. "What did you do to my room?"

"I cleaned it," Scarlet said. "What a dump! I found chocolate milk cartons under the bed that expired a year ago."

"You didn't have to take down my Don Ho poster," I said, staring at the blank spot on the wall.

"I didn't like that weird guy staring at me," Scarlet said. "Who's Don Ho?"

"Only the greatest interpreter of Hawaiian tiki lounge music who ever lived." Didn't she know anything?

"I don't really care," she said. "If I don't get this horrible stuff out of my hair right now, I'm going to scream."

"Don't scream," I said. "I'm not a screamer, and it will make Mom nervous and Rosemary more suspicious. Come on, the bathroom's across the hall."

I led Scarlet to the bathroom and helped her wash her hair over the sink. Mom had bought me a special disinfectant shampoo just for mishaps like this.

"Thank you." Scarlet wrapped a towel around her head, turban style. I'd always wondered how to do that. "I feel better now." She sat on the bed, which had been neatly made for the first time in about five years.

I sat next to her. "Well, I don't. It creeps me out to think of you rummaging around in my room, *cleaning* and *straightening things up*." I shuddered.

"That wasn't what I meant when I said I felt better," she snapped. "You think I like living in this pigsty?"

"At least my room has character." I was used to defending my pigsty against Mom, and I could be very touchy about it. "*Your* room looks like Barbie lives in it. Like a plastic dream house."

At the word *plastic*, she winced. "It's not plastic, it's *clean*," she insisted, truly mad at me now. "It's a million times nicer than this dump, and you know it."

Maybe, maybe not, but she'd never get me to admit it. "Let's get down to business," I said. "We're the victims of some kind of weird syndrome and we've got to figure out a way to switch our bodies back."

"That's the first thing you've said all day that makes sense." She paused. "What should we do first?"

I shrugged. "Start searching online, I guess."

I opened my laptop and we checked out "body swapping." That turned up a lot of links to TV shows and a few spells.

"Let's try one of these spells," Scarlet said.

I read the one she pointed to. "That's the lamest spell ever. That will never work."

"How do you know? We might as well try it."

I sighed and read the instructions out loud as Scarlet prepared the spell. "Step one: Close your eyes."

She closed her eyes. "You have to close yours too."

"How can I read the instructions if my eyes are closed?"

"Okay — after you read them. What's next?"

"Step two: Relax." She leaned against the pillows of my bed, breathing deeply. I couldn't help it — this bugged me. "I don't know how you can relax at a time like this," I said.

Her eyes flew open. "You just told me to relax!"

"I know, but . . . never mind." I looked at the instructions. "Step three: Think of the person you want to switch with."

Scarlet stared at me with deep concentration. Then she closed her eyes again. "I'm thinking of you. It isn't pleasant. Next?"

"Step four: Believe it will work."

"I believe," she said. "I believe this will work."

"Step five: Hope it will work." I shook my head. "See, here's where the spell really loses me. *Hope* it will work? That doesn't give me much confidence. . . ."

"Be quiet and keep reading."

"Step six: Go to sleep. When you wake up, you will be in the body you were thinking of. Warning: This doesn't always work." I sighed.

"You have to do it too," Scarlet said. "Believe! You're not believing. I can tell. You're not even *hoping*."

"Oh, I'm hoping. But I'm not believing. When a spell warns you that it won't work, it's pretty hard to take it seriously."

She sat up. "We can't fall asleep right now anyway. You have to go to my house and work Mom's party."

"I'm not doing that."

"You have to."

"Not if I can find a way to get back into my body. Then *you'll* have to work your mom's stupid party."

"Gladly," Scarlet said. "Anything's better than this."

She didn't have to be so mean about it. I started scrolling through the search listings, looking for something else that might help us. I found a lot of strange information about curses, trances, hypnosis, herbal cures, even weird diseases, but no answers to our immediate problem.

"Let's talk this through," Scarlet said. "When did you first notice that you were me?"

"When I woke up this morning."

"Me too." She shuddered. "That was a horrible moment."

"Hey, I wasn't so thrilled either," I said. "That hot pink in your room nearly burned out my retinas."

She ignored me. "So yesterday was our birthday. *Both* of our birthdays. That can't be a coincidence. We must have done something to trigger the body switch. But what?"

We tried to figure it out for a good ten minutes. It felt like hours. Mom brought the grilled cheeses and some lemonade and left us to work on our "project." I'd never seen her so polite. I think she was afraid if she made one wrong move, her lovely new daughter would turn back into a pumpkin and her lovely new daughter's even lovelier new friend would disappear.

If only it were that easy.

"Maybe there's something about turning thirteen," Scarlet said. "After all, it's an unlucky number."

"But then, why wouldn't this happen to everyone else when *they* turn thirteen?" I asked. "I don't think Zoe switched bodies with anyone in our class on her birthday. If anything, she switched with Cruella De Vil."

"Hey, that's my best friend you're talking about," Scarlet said.

I snorted. "Some best friend."

Scarlet frowned. "Well, she's nice to *me*."

I considered disputing that but decided to keep my mouth shut on the subject. We chewed our sandwiches and thought some more.

"Was there something unusual that happened to both of us yesterday?" I said. "Or something out of the ordinary that we both did?"

"Let's go over every minute," Scarlet said.

We went over the day in painful detail. The contrast between her birthday and mine was brought back to me in full force. I really didn't need to relive the horror again.

"Believe me, nothing that happened to you in school was the same as what happened to me," I said.

"All right. Last night. What did your mother make for dinner?"

We went over all the presents we got, what the cards said, the food we ate, where we ate it. None of it was the same. Until we got to —

"The cake," Scarlet said. "What kind did you have?"

"Devil's food," I said. "With pink icing. Store-bought." Mom must have been busy that day because she usually baked our birthday cakes herself.

"Wait a minute," Scarlet said. "I had devil's food cake too. With pink frosting."

We were getting somewhere. We could feel it.

"Did you have thirteen candles?" I asked.

"No," she said. "I had one candle. Orange. Shaped like the number thirteen."

I grabbed her. "I had that candle too!"

"That must be it!" she said. "It's the only detail we both share."

"Maybe that's what did it," I said. "The cake and the candle. Or one of them. Let's ask Mom where she got them."

We went down to the kitchen. Rosemary was gone, doing homework in her room. Mom was starting supper. Corned beef and cabbage.

"Mom —" I said before I realized what I was doing. My hand flew to my mouth. Mom turned around smiled. She thought Scarlet was talking to her.

"Mom," Scarlet said, taking over, "where did you get the cake and candle we had last night on my birthday?"

"Did you like it?" Mom asked. "I can try to get the same kind of cake tomorrow —"

"Sure, it was great," Scarlet said. "Where did it come from?"

"You mean, where did I buy it?" Mom said. "At the ValueMart, of course."

"In the bakery section?" I pressed.

"That's the funny thing," Mom said. "It wasn't in the bakery section at all. I was wandering down the Household Cleansers and Pet Food aisle, looking for Handi Wipes, when I came across this little booth. One of those temporary promotional booths companies set up sometimes. It was decorated with orange paper flames and they were selling devil's food cakes and candles. They only had number thirteen candles, for some reason. They were out of all the other numbers."

"Did the company have a name?" Scarlet asked.

"It must have, but I don't remember," Mom said. "Why all the questions?"

"No reason," I said. "We were just curious, that's all."

"Yes, but why? You didn't seem so enthusiastic about the cake last night."

I'd felt she was trying to tell me something by giving me a pink cake. But I didn't say anything about that now.

Scarlet pulled me through the kitchen toward the back door. "We're going out for a ride now, okay?" she told my mom.

"Sure, honey. Be careful. And don't be late for supper."

"I won't," Scarlet said. "Bye."

We went out to the garage, hopped on my bike and Rosemary's, and pedaled as fast as we could to the ValueMart on Coldspring Lane.

"We've got to get that candle," Scarlet said. "That must be the secret. Did you hear what your mom said? They only had number thirteen? That's pretty weird."

"It's the best lead we have," I said.

It was strange to watch Scarlet up ahead of me, riding my

bike in my body. Strange to see how I sat on a bike, how I pedalled. I looked kind of like a duck, if I was honest with myself. A duck on a bike. For some reason I flapped my feet when I pedalled. If I ever got my body back, maybe I'd try to cut that out.

We parked our bikes and ran into the store. I knew exactly where the Household Cleansers were — Mom's favorite aisle. Aisle Five.

We walked down Aisle Five, scanning the rows of bottles and cans and bags of dog kibble. There was no booth selling cake. No desserts of any kind.

"It's gone," Scarlet said.

Just to be sure, we scoured the rest of the store in search of devil's food cake and candles. We found plenty of cake, and some of the cakes had pink icing, but they weren't the same. And the only candles they had were the regular kind, not the numeral-carved-in-wax kind. We even asked at the bakery counter and the guy working there said the store was out of them.

We trudged out of the supermarket, discouraged.

"Now what are we going to do?" Scarlet asked.

"What about your house?" I said. "Could we find any clues there?"

"I don't think so. I had my cake at a restaurant. We left the box and the candle and everything there. They must have thrown it all out by now."

"My candle didn't burn all the way down," I said. "Maybe we can still find the stub in the trash."

70

"So now we have to dig through the garbage?" Scarlet said. "Ew."

"Don't be such a wimp. Maybe there was some kind of sticker on the candle, with the name of the company that makes it. That could help us figure out what's going on."

She pedaled wearily. "Yeah, but digging through the garbage . . ."

We left our bikes in the garage, where the big trash cans were. From the smell I could tell the garbage hadn't been picked up recently.

I opened one can, Scarlet opened the other, and we started digging. She gingerly picked through the scraps of paper and bits of food, wrinkling her nose at the smell. Even though she was in my body, she didn't really look much like me. That was not the way I handled garbage. She glanced at me bent over the trash can, digging frantically.

"Hey — watch the manicure," she snapped.

I rolled my eyes. "Our lives are at stake, and you're worried about your nails?"

"I just polished them."

Under a pile of orange rinds I spotted something soapy-white. I snatched it up. A wax stub. I could just make out the bottom of the one and the three.

"I've got it!" I said.

"Hooray!" Scarlet cried out.

We studied the candle. I brushed away a bit of pink frosting. The wick had burned away completely.

A stamp on the bottom said MADE IN KALAMAZOO.

"What does that mean?" Scarlet asked.

"It means there's something rotten in the state of Michigan," I said. "And we're going to find out what."

Back in my room, we searched the Internet for candle manufacturers in Kalamazoo and found nothing useful. Instead we found out that the Michigan state motto was "*Si quaeris peninsulam amoenam, circumspice*," which is Latin for "If you see a pleasant peninsula, look around you."

"What are we going to do?" I wailed. "How can a candle say *Made in Kalamazoo* if nobody in Kalamazoo makes candles?"

"I don't know." Scarlet rubbed the stub of wax. "We'll just have to keep looking."

"But the auditions are tomorrow! For *The Music Man*! What if we don't switch back by then?"

"I don't know," Scarlet said. "But I'm auditioning no matter what."

I took the candle stub from her and rubbed it like a genie's lamp, wishing, wishing, wishing. Nothing happened.

"It's hopeless." Scarlet's lower lip quivered. "We're stuck like this forever."

"We can't be," I said. "We'll find a way out of this. Somehow." Then I remembered something Mr. Brummel had said the day before — something about his school days in Kalamazoo.

"Wait a minute," I said. "Isn't Mr. Brummel from Kalamazoo?"

"Is he?" Scarlet said. "I don't know."

"Maybe he knows something about these candles." I glanced at the clock. "The auditions for A through L are this afternoon — they weren't starting until after the soccer game and other extracurriculars were over. He might still be at school if the auditions went long. I could go ask him —"

"You can't," Scarlet said. "You have to go home and help my mother with her dinner party."

"Who cares about that?" I said. "This is a matter of life and death!"

"To my mother, a dinner party *is* a matter of life and death," Scarlet said. "If you don't show up, there will be a huge scene. Steve will threaten to take away your phone; Ben will lurk around snickering and teasing you; and Mom will sit there sniffling like she's about to have a nervous breakdown. And it will be all your fault."

"That's an experience I'd rather avoid," I said.

"You don't want to push Mom over the edge," Scarlet told me. "I'll find Mr. Brummel and ask him what he knows. Your mom won't mind, right?"

"Well, if you tell her it's for school . . ." I really wanted to find Mr. Brummel myself. "I don't want to be the cause of someone's nervous breakdown. You go. But call me right away and tell me what Mr. Brummel says."

"I will. I promise," she said.

"And don't tell him the whole story," I said. "I mean, about the switching and everything. Unless you have to. But try not to."

"I won't," Scarlet said. "I don't want people to know about this any more than you do."

10

Ya Got Trouble

I zipped to school on Lavender's bike and burst into the auditorium. Mr. Brummel sat in front of the stage, watching Masha Llewellyn screech out a song in front of a few stragglers. I'd just made it.

It had been strange to watch Lavender dig through the garbage in my body. I recognized the outer shell, but it didn't look like *me* somehow. Those were my pink nails (already chipped), my frowning face, my long hair brushing against a banana peel (ew!), but Lavender's blunt energy changed everything. I thought it would be like looking at myself in the mirror, but it was more like watching myself in a dream, one of those dreams where everything looks a little different from the way it looks in real life, but it's hard to say exactly how.

Her room was more bearable now that I'd cleaned it up, but it still had a funny smell. It wasn't a bad smell, exactly. It was just unfamiliar. It didn't smell like my house. I liked her mother, though. She was warm, one of those people everybody likes — everybody except Lavender, I guess.

I slipped into the back row to wait out the last auditions of *A* through *L*. Charlie Scott sat at the other end of the row. He waved to me. I scooted over to him.

"What are you doing here?" I asked. "Our auditions aren't until tomorrow."

"I know," Charlie said. "I just wanted to check out the competition."

Whoa. He was really serious about this.

"What about you?" he asked.

"Oh, um . . . I just need to talk to Mr. Brummel for a minute."

"You don't have to worry, Lavender," Charlie said. "None of the girls who tried out today blew me away."

"That's good to know," I said. I couldn't tell him that the audition was far from my only worry.

"I think you'd be a great Marian," Charlie said.

"Really?" I didn't know what else to say. Charlie wanted Lavender to get the lead? What about me?

"You know who else is really good?" I said. "Scarlet Martinez. I think she'd be perfect. She was, like, born to play Marian Paree."

"Paroo," Charlie said. "It's Marian Paroo."

"Right. Paroo."

"Don't you want the part?" Charlie asked.

"Sure I do," I said. "I just think, you know, if *I* don't get it, Scarlet would be good."

"Well, I've never seen her onstage," Charlie said. "But she's very pretty."

I blushed. I nearly said, "Thank you," but stopped myself just in time.

"Is something wrong?" Charlie asked. "Your face just turned red."

"No," I said. "Everything's great."

"I didn't mean that Scarlet would make a better Marian than you," Charlie said. "I think you'd be good too."

"I know," I said. "You don't have to apologize."

"I didn't mean to hurt your feelings."

He took my blushing all wrong. He thought I was mad instead of flattered. How cute of him.

"You didn't hurt my feelings, I swear," I said. "I actually kind of *hope* Scarlet gets the lead. For the good of the production."

Charlie shook his head. "Wow, Lavender. It's great to know that someone cares about the play as much as I do. You've really got the true spirit of the theater in you."

"Thanks." I blushed again. But wait: Who had the true spirit of the theater in her — me or Lavender? Between all the blushing and the confusion, my head was getting woozy. "Scarlet's very serious about the theater too."

"I didn't know that," Charlie said. "I've never heard her talk about it before."

"Oh yes. She's a real hoofer." Was that a theater word? I didn't know. Maybe it wasn't, because Charlie looked confused.

"Hoofer?"

"Is that not a word?"

"It means 'dancer.'"

"Oh." I was an okay dancer, but I wouldn't want to claim any special talent in it. "I meant something else." Rats, why didn't I know more about the theater? I sounded like an idiot.

"Trouper?" Charlie suggested.

"Yeah. Scarlet is a real trouper."

"When did you and Scarlet get so close?" Charlie asked. "I didn't know you were friends."

"Friends?" Uh-oh. "Well, we've, you know, *bonded* recently. Very recently. In the last day or two."

"That's cool. Some of the kids in this school are so cliquish, you know? Like, just because someone's a little different from them, they have to make a big point of being mean about it."

"Oh, yeah, I definitely know what you're talking about," I said, a bit nervously.

"People say mean things about other people all the time," Charlie said. "They even make up total lies! It's unbelievable."

"Unbelievable." I shifted a bit in my seat. I didn't like where this conversation was headed.

"So I'm glad to hear that Scarlet isn't like that," Charlie said. "I didn't think she was, but, you know, she hangs out with Zoe and Kelsey, so —"

"Yeah, Zoe and Kelsey, those girls, well . . . ha,

they're, like, capable of anything." I hoped he didn't notice how hot my face was.

"Anyway, Lavender, I hope you know that the rest of us don't listen to the crazy stuff those girls say."

Gulp. Now it was *really* time to change the subject. "Which song are you going to sing for your audition?" I asked.

"I haven't decided yet," Charlie replied. "What about you? Which *Music Man* song is your favorite?"

"My favorite?" I didn't know any of the songs yet. I'd been planning to play Lavender's sound track that night when I got back to her house, on that weird record player thing that she had in her room. "Um, I like the one that goes 'Doo doo doo, doo doo doo.'" I hummed a vague melody, hoping he'd magically hear a real tune somewhere in there.

"Which one is that?"

"It's, you know, 'Doo doo doo, doo doo doo —'"

"Oh — you mean 'Seventy-Six Trombones'?"

"Exactly!" I said. "I love that song."

"That is a good one. 'Ya Got Trouble' is fun to sing too."

"'Ya Got Trouble.' Yeah."

The last singer finished her song. Mr. Brummel closed the piano lid and packed up his music. I was relieved — I couldn't keep up this bluffing much longer.

"I'd better catch Mr. Brummel before he leaves," I said.

"See you tomorrow, Lavender," Charlie said. "And don't worry — you'll be great."

I had to remind myself again that Charlie wasn't really talking to me — he thought he was talking to Lavender. But I couldn't help but wish he was saying these words to me. And meaning them.

"Thanks!" I would have tried to get a few more sentences out of him about how great I was, but I really had to act fast. I dashed up the aisle. "Mr. Brummel! Can I talk to you for a second?"

"Hello, Lavender," Mr. Brummel said. "What can I do for you?"

"Um —" How to put it without giving away my secret? "Did I hear you say you're from Kalamazoo?"

This was *not* the question he was expecting. "Yes," he said after a moment of no doubt wondering why I was asking. "I grew up there."

"Kalamazoo, Michigan?"

"I believe that's the only Kalamazoo on the map," Mr. Brummel said. "What's this about?"

"Well, I turned thirteen yesterday —"

"That's right! I saw you and Scarlet celebrating in the hall. Did you have a happy birthday?"

"It was okay for a while . . ." I began. "And then it turned weird."

"Weird? Hmm. What happened?"

He was smiling at me in a funny way, and I couldn't figure out why. Did he think something was wrong with me? Could he tell that he was not really talking to Lavender, but to me?

"Um, well, I guess the only weird thing that happened was that the candle on my birthday cake came from Kalamazoo. And I really liked that candle. Do you know where I could find another one? They're all out of them at the ValueMart. I even tried to order one off the Internet, but I couldn't find any information on the Kalamazoo candle industry."

"Hmm," Mr. Brummel said. "That sounds very mysterious."

"Exactly! It's *very* mysterious."

"But I have a feeling the mystery of the candle is not the real issue here. Are you worried about your audition, Lavender?" Mr. Brummel started down the aisle toward the door. I trotted along beside him. The auditorium was deserted now. I wished there had been some reason for Charlie to stay.

"It's not that so much. It's —"

"Because you have nothing to worry about," Mr. Brummel said. "I understand you're nervous. But you're talented, and you've got guts. . . ."

"But —"

"Just make sure you know the character," he said. "Through and through. That's the key."

"I will, but —"

"*Through and through.* Go home, brush up on your audition song, and I'll see you tomorrow afternoon." We walked outside to the parking lot. Mr. Brummel opened his car door. "Okay?"

"Okay."

I watched him drive away. Then I got on my bike and rode north toward Goodwood Gardens. I was halfway to my house when I remembered I had to go to 34th Street — where Lavender lived — instead.

For a moment I thought of her at my house, with Steve and Mom and Mom's party.

I almost — *almost* — felt sorry for her. And relieved for me.

II

Cat Brains on a Cracker

I took my time getting back to Scarlet's house, and still made it back by seven. Ben sat at the kitchen island playing Nintendo. Scarlet's mother was spraying Windex on the brass cabinet handles. As if they weren't already blinding.

"Scarlet, you're filthy! Go take a shower right this instant!" she said. No *Hello*, no *How was your day?* or *Did you win the soccer game?*

On second thought, it was probably better that she didn't ask about the soccer game.

"Hurry up!" she added. "The Mortensons will be here in an hour. And don't touch the kitchen cupboards. I just cleaned them."

"What if I want a snack?" I asked.

"A snack!" was the only response I got to that.

"The Leech spazzed on her game today," Ben announced. "Even her friends were chewing her out."

"Who asked you?" I snapped.

The last thing I wanted to think about was soccer. Not that I cared, but I hadn't ruined the game on purpose. I'd tried to kick the ball to my teammates. Was it my fault that the other team's players got in the way?

"That reminds me, Scarlet," her mother said. "You left your phone on the counter. You've been getting texts all afternoon."

I picked up the phone she was talking about and looked at it blankly.

"Take it upstairs," Scarlet's mother said. "And get in that shower."

I walked slowly up the stairs, looking at the phone. There were ten frantic texts from Zoe: *Where are you? Call me! What's up? Why are you acting so weird?* — that sort of thing.

I went into Scarlet's room and gasped again at its luxury. Scarlet had a suite all to herself: very big, with a deck overlooking the backyard, and a private bathroom with a shower *and* a Jacuzzi. I filled the Jacuzzi and got in, trying to relax. Her phone jangled. Zoe again.

"I can't talk now," I said. "I'm busy."

"This will only take a sec," Zoe said. "You hurried away from the field so fast we didn't have a chance to do a post-game analysis."

"Can't it wait?" I said.

"No," said another voice.

"Who's that?" I asked.

"It's Kelsey," Zoe said. "We're three-way-calling you."

"What was wrong with you today?" Kelsey demanded. "Did you have a brain injury?"

"You'd better not play like that next week," Zoe said. "It's our last chance to make the finals."

"If we lose, you'll be more unpopular than Lavender Schmitz," Kelsey said.

"I don't know about *that*," Zoe said. "Scarlet could never be less popular than Lavender. She'd have to, like, grow a hump on her back and have reverse plastic surgery to make her uglier, plus spray some kind of stink perfume all over her —"

"Hey, cut it out," I said.

"What, do you *like* Lavender?" Zoe said. "Then you really *do* have a brain injury."

"Um, no," I said carefully. "Of course I don't like her. I just think it's mean to talk about other people that way."

Zoe snorted. "Since when?"

"Since now," I said. "I have to go."

"Watch some game tapes," Zoe said. "And take some vitamins or something."

"I don't care about soccer, anyway," I said. "I'm going to audition for the musical tomorrow."

"What?" Zoe cracked up. "You were serious about that?"

"I thought you were kidding," Kelsey said.

"I'm not kidding," I told them.

"This I've got to see," Zoe said.

"Why?" I asked. "Is there a problem?"

They kept laughing. Clearly they knew something I didn't.

"I've got to go," I said, and hung up.

How bad could it be? As far as I could tell, people applauded no matter what Scarlet did. Well, as long as she wasn't spoiling a soccer game . . .

. . . which, I thought, Zoe and Kelsey didn't have to be so cranky about. Weren't they Scarlet's best friends? Where was the love? The support? The friendly encouragement?

If I, as Lavender, had screwed up a soccer game, many of my classmates would have booed me and thrown things on the field. But Maybelle would have tried to cheer me up.

Maybelle. I missed her. I'd seen her in the halls during the day, but couldn't figure out a reason to say hello to her that didn't seem too strange.

Now I was left with Zoe and Kelsey, who I didn't like anyway.

I put their sneering out of my mind. All I cared about was playing Marian the Librarian in the school musical. Zoe and Kelsey could laugh about it all they wanted.

Scarlet's mother burst into the bedroom. "Aren't you ready yet?" she shouted to me in the bathroom. "I'm picking out a dress for you to wear and leaving it on your bed."

That was fine with me. I wouldn't have known what to pick anyway.

"And honey," Scarlet's mother added, "please, please try to get along with Ben tonight. Don't pick a fight with him in front of the Mortensons, okay? I want them to see what a happy family we are."

"I won't pick a fight with Ben," I said. "But what if he picks a fight with me?"

She appeared in the doorway, frowning. I sank a little lower beneath the bubbles.

"Don't be smart," she said. "It takes two to tango."

"Okay," I said. "I'll be good."

"When you come downstairs I expect a smile on your face and your best manners."

"Don't worry, I'll smile."

She left. I got out of the tub — nice soft towels, brand new, with no worn patches — and got dressed. Scarlet's mom had picked out a white dress with a ruffle across the neckline. Yech.

I had a feeling pretending to be a happy family wasn't going to be easy. And that white dress didn't help one bit.

"Canape?" I dipped the tray low so Mrs. Mortenson could take an hors d'oeuvre.

"Scarlet, aren't you lovely," Mrs. Mortenson said. Her hand hovered over the tray. "These look delicious. What are they?"

I brought the tray close to my face, studying the little round thing she'd pointed to. It was a tiny orange cracker covered with brownish-gray goo.

"I don't know," I said. "Looks like cat brains to me."

Mrs. Mortenson looked startled, then laughed. She thought I was kidding. I wasn't.

"It does look like some kind of organ meat, doesn't it?" she said. "Could be pâté. Is your mother getting trendy on us? How offal!"

I had no idea what she was talking about, so I shrugged, which tilted the tray. Several canapes slid to the floor, detouring to brush against my white dress and leave three little brown splotches.

Steve and Mr. Mortenson laughed. "Good one, dear," Mr. Mortenson said. "Offal, o-f-f-a-l. Get it, Scarlet?"

I didn't. But I smiled like my "mom" had told me to and pretended it was the funniest thing I'd ever heard.

When he was done laughing, Steve saw the brown stains on my dress and shook his head in disgust, just slightly. He didn't think I noticed, but I did.

Ben laughed his head off and slapped his knee — so much that I wondered if he'd really understood the joke, or if he was just faking. Probably faking. He was sitting on the couch next to Mr. Mortenson, drinking a ginger ale, stuffing his face with chips, and trying to sound intelligent while talking to the adults, which meant no talking about video games, or sci-fi movies, or anything else that actually interested him. Steve watched him out of the corner of his eye, and Ben glanced nervously in Steve's direction every once in a while, as if checking to make sure he was doing okay. I didn't envy him, but still: Why didn't *he* have to serve the guests too?

"I can't eat garlic powder," Mrs. Mortenson said. "Will you ask Leigh if there's any garlic powder in this?"

"Who's Leigh?" I asked.

Mrs. Mortenson got that startled look again, which segued into another laugh.

"You don't know your own mother's name?"

"Oh — *Leigh*," I said. "Sorry. I just think of her as Mom."

Note to self: Scarlet's mom's name is Leigh.

The tray slipped again, and I lost three more hors d'oeuvres. I bent down to pick them up. Steve watched me, annoyed.

"Scarlet, what's the matter with you tonight?" he said.

"Let me help you, Scarlet," Mrs. Mortenson said. She leaned over and picked up a few of the fallen cat brains. As she sat up again, her head bumped against the tray. *Clang!* The whole thing went *splat* against my chest.

"Oh, dear, I'm so sorry!" she cried.

"It's not your fault, Sheila," Steve said. "Scarlet must have left her mind upstairs in her room tonight."

Scarlet's mom — *Leigh* — breezed in. "Dinner's almost ready." She saw me and grimaced. "*Scarlet!* What happened to your dress?"

I looked down. It was splotched with brown goo.

"Um —"

"Go upstairs and change. We're eating in five minutes."

While I trudged upstairs I heard her say to the Mortensons, "She's been going through a phase lately. I just don't get it. Where's my sweet little ballerina gone?"

"It happened to Emily too," Mrs. Mortenson said. "They hit thirteen and suddenly you don't recognize them anymore."

I shut the door to my room, pulled off my food-stained dress, and lay on the bed for a short rest.

Being Scarlet was tiring.

"Scarlet!" Her mom called my name in a voice I recognized — a voice you used when company was around. Nice silvery tone camouflaging severe annoyance.

"Coming!" I yelled back. I felt like throwing on a pair of sweats but knew that would only get me sent back to change again. I picked out a black dress that was close in style to the white one. At least the black would hide stains better.

But Scarlet's mom frowned when I presented myself in the kitchen. "You know how I feel about young girls in black," she whispered. "It's too sophisticated. What are you trying to prove?"

"Nothing," I said.

"Put on the pink eyelet," she told me.

"Sure thing," I said, even though I had no idea what the heck an eyelet was.

Back in the bedroom, I found a pink dress with little holes punched in it. *This had better be an eyelet*, I thought. I put it on, went back downstairs, and this time got a grim nod of approval.

We ate in the dining room, which overlooked the big back yard. All the food was shiny and arranged — designed more than cooked. There were glazed miniature chickens — Mrs. Mortenson called them *Cornish game hens* — vegetables that looked like little iced cakes, and mounds of rice shaped into footballs. Fussy. But I was hungry, so I ate while the adults talked about whose house was for sale and how much the owners were asking.

Once the real estate conversation was over, Mr. Mortenson asked, "How's school this year, Ben?"

Ben put down his fork and finished chewing his game hen. There was an awkward moment of silence while we waited for him to swallow. Steve cleared his throat.

"Ben's doing okay," Steve said. "If he spent less time

playing video games and more time studying, he'd be at the top of his class. Probably."

Ben looked down at his plate and tapped his fork on a chicken bone. Steve reached over and stopped his hand. Ben lifted his head, miserable, and I caught his eye.

"How about you, Scarlet?" Mrs. Mortenson asked. "Having a good school year?"

No, I thought, though by now I knew better than to say so. It hadn't taken me long to get the hang of this family.

"I'm doing fine," I said.

"What grade are you in?"

"Eighth."

"She's the star of the soccer team," Scarlet's mom said.

Ben laughed.

"What's so funny?" Steve asked.

"You should have seen Scarlet play today," Ben said. "Every time she got the ball, the other side scored!"

I thought it *was* kind of funny, now that it was over with.

But Steve didn't find it funny at all. "Is that true?" he asked.

"I was having an off day," I explained.

Scarlet's mom stared at me. "But Scarlet, you told me . . ."

"I told you what?" I said.

"You told us you were the best player on the team," Steve said.

"And of course you'd take her word for it," Ben said. "Never having been to one of her games yourself."

It hadn't even occurred to me before to wonder why her

parents hadn't been there today. But now it seemed that wasn't unusual at all. I couldn't believe it.

They'd never even seen her play soccer.

I couldn't help defending her. "I *am* the best player," I said. "You can read it in the school newspaper. Ask my coach. I just had *a bad day*."

I didn't know how long I'd be in Scarlet's body. What if I had to spend the rest of my life with these people? The sooner they learned to stop hassling me, the happier we'd all be.

"Look," I went on, "if you don't believe me, why don't you try coming to one of my games and see for yourselves?"

Scarlet's mom dropped her jaw, then her fork. The Mortensons were openly staring at us now. Ben looked stunned, and maybe a little pleased. Steve stood up, his big blockhead face set to ANGRY.

"Young lady, you don't speak to your mother that way."

"I was talking to both of you," I said. "I can't believe you haven't watched your own daughter play her favorite sport."

Scarlet's mom's eyes were all wet and quaky.

Oh help, I thought. *What have I done now?*

"We gave you that wonderful birthday dinner last night," she said through choked-back sobs. "And all those presents. The ballet lessons, the piano lessons, soccer camp, the tutors . . . and that's not enough for you?"

"That's all fine," I said. "Great. Terrific. Look, if you're too busy to come to my games, just say so."

"Go to your room!" Steve conveniently pointed the way for me. "Right now."

I gobbled up a big forkful of rice before standing up to go. "Gladly." A few grains of rice dribbled off my lip and onto my pink *eyelet* dress.

I didn't care, and wanted them to see I didn't care.

I had more important things on my mind.

12

Your Chicken Pot Pie Is Going Down

"More pancakes, Lav?"

Lavender's mother reloaded my plate before I could say no. Her father and sister sat stuffing their faces while her mother churned out more and more food.

"You're not eating your scrapple," Mrs. Lavender said. "You usually love scrapple."

So that's what scrapple was: a rectangular sausage-like substance. Scrapple. It looked as gross as it sounded.

"Are you still feeling sick?" Lavender's mother asked.

I had told them I felt sick the night before, after seeing Mr. Brummel. Then I'd locked myself in my room with a bag of popcorn and searched the Internet for a way to get my body back. I didn't find anything helpful. I'd once thought you could find out anything on the Internet, but it turned out to be an unreliable resource for magic spells.

"I'm feeling better," I reported. Except for my stomach, which was bursting with pancakes. "But I don't want any scrapple. I need to be light on my feet today. I've got that audition this afternoon."

Lavender's mother kissed me — *again*. She was always kissing and hugging and squeezing and cheek-rubbing and *mm-mmm!*-ing. I didn't know how to respond to that. My mom's tendency to do that kind of thing had left when my dad did. So it had been a while.

"I'm so glad you decided to audition for that musical," Lavender's mother said. "You'll make lots of new friends, like that nice girl Scarlet."

"You'll get the part," Lavender's father said. "What's the role? The librarian? Look at you! You're a librarian if I ever saw one."

Uh, thanks? Considering what I was working with, I thought I looked pretty good. I couldn't help it if Lavender had no taste in clothes. I'd only found one decent thing in Lavender's room, and it was an accessory: a brand-new bag from Maroc, with a long strap and lots of buckles. So I had a cool bag and nothing to wear with it.

"What are you going to do for your audition?" Rosemary asked. "Play your ukulele?"

"What? No," I snapped. "I'm not stupid."

"That's a funny thing to say," Lavender's mother observed. "Not that *I'm* so crazy about it, but you love your uke."

"Sure, but other people think it's dorky." How could Lavender's parents not see that? It was so obvious.

"But *you* don't," Rosemary said, looking at me funny again.

"Um, I mean, um . . ." How did the real Lavender

talk to them? I hadn't figured it out yet. "I've got to get to school."

I pushed away from the table and slung the Maroc bag over my shoulder.

Lavender's mother gasped and clapped her hand over her mouth. You'd think I'd just said I was off to Mars and would be late for supper.

"What?" I asked.

"Lavender — the purse," her mother said. "You're wearing . . . the purse?"

I checked to make sure it wasn't leaking blood or something. "Yeah, why not?"

"You told us you hated the purse, that's why not," Lavender's father said.

"I did? But it's a great bag," I said. What was wrong with Lavender? I wished *I'd* gotten a bag like this for my birthday . . . in addition to all the other awesome stuff I'd gotten.

Lavender's mother pressed her palm against my forehead. "I'm afraid you're still under the weather."

"What have you done with my sister?" Rosemary asked.

I brushed my mother's hand away. "I'm fine. Can I please go to school now?"

"Sure, honey. Of course. Good luck with your audition."

"Break a leg, baby doll," Lavender's father shouted as I hurried out the door.

That morning was as bad as the morning before. It was hard to decide which part was the worst, but a strong contender was definitely the tripping. I tripped down the steps of Lavender's house. I tripped over three cracks in the sidewalk. I tripped up the steps to school. Once inside I thought I'd be okay, since the school halls are fairly straight and even, but no. People seemed to stick their feet out wherever I went, just to watch me trip over them.

I found Lavender at my locker before the first bell. We'd typed up our homework and now we swapped it — even though we were in different sections of most classes, the basic material was the same. However, she still had to go to French first period. And we were having a quiz. I'd been hoping to get an A in French, but if Lavender took my quizzes, I didn't have a chance.

"I meant to tutor you in conjugating verbs last night!" I whispered urgently. "I totally forgot."

The bell rang.

"Too late now," Lavender said.

"No! Listen! *Aller: vais, vas, va, allons, allez, vont . . .*"

"Give it up, Scarlet. There's no hope. I'm going to flunk that quiz."

"No! I've got to pass. Maybe you can copy off of someone. Madame Geller is pretty out of it. Try to sit next to Masha."

Lavender looked shocked. "I'm not a cheater."

"Neither am I, but this is so not fair. . . ."

"What if I get caught?"

"Don't! Please don't get caught! That would be worse than flunking."

The second bell rang. "We're going to be late," Lavender said. "Oh — by the way, I — or, I mean, you — are giving a demonstration in science today on how insects are a good source of protein, and I promised Barbash I'd eat a cricket. You know those crickets he keeps to feed to the frogs? So get ready to eat a cricket this morning. Hey, why is your face so white?"

I felt sick. "I'm not doing that," I said.

"Fine. Then I'm not cheating on your French quiz."

"Fine."

"Fine."

"Girls, get to class." Ms. Judson, the principal, was patrolling the halls for stragglers. "You're late."

I hurried off to English class. Ms. Kantner was talking about the problem of mistaken identity in *The Prince and the Pauper*, a book I loved, but I hardly listened. I was too busy trying to think of a way to avoid eating a cricket next period. Stupid Lavender.

I passed Lavender in the hall on the way to science. "How was the French quiz?" I asked.

She gave me the thumbs-down. "Remember, with the cricket — don't chew, just swallow it whole. Unless you like your bugs crunchy . . ."

I wanted to cry.

Mr. Barbash greeted me with a big grin when I walked into the Science Lab. "Lavender! Ready for your demonstration?"

"Uh, Mr. Barbash, I've been thinking —"

"Not going to back out, are you? That's not the Lavender I know. Always up for anything!"

"Never afraid to make a fool of herself," I muttered.

"That's the spirit!"

I was hit with inspiration at the last possible second. "Mr. Barbash, I really wanted to eat that cricket, but I can't."

"Why not?"

"I just found out I'm allergic to crickets. If I eat one, my throat will swell up. I could die."

I enjoyed watching the blood drain from his face. "That's terrible! Then you absolutely shouldn't do it. Are you allergic to flies too?"

"Definitely."

"Sorry to hear that. Well, you'll just have to make your presentation without it."

Right. Something about insects and protein. Which I knew nothing about. I made something up, which seemed to satisfy Mr. Barbash. My classmates didn't care what I said. They paid no attention except when Mr. Barbash's back was turned and Zach Griffith slingshotted paper clips at me.

I made it through the morning without having to eat a bug. But that wasn't the end of my troubles.

In gym we played dodgeball. I tried to dodge, I really did. But Lavender seemed to be everyone's favorite target. After twenty minutes of that, I was black and blue.

Then came lunch. At first I felt relief, because in my old life lunch was easy. But this was Lavender's lunch, a different lunch period from mine, and lunch was definitely the worst part of Lavender's day.

"Lavender! Over here!" Zoe waved to me from her — our — table in the corner by the window. She patted the seat next to her, as if she wanted me to sit there.

I started toward the table, forgetting for a second who I was. Then I remembered — I was Lavender. Zoe never invited Lavender to sit with her.

What was she up to?

I scanned the cafeteria for another free seat. The place was packed. The only spots open were at the jock-boy table — no way, I wasn't asking for trouble — or with the Pimple Poppers. They were really called the Roswell Club in Defense of Alien Life. We — Zoe, Kelsey, and me — nicknamed them the Pimple Poppers because the one thing they all had in common, besides their belief in UFOs, was a bad complexion.

"Lavender!" Zoe waved to me again, this time with Kelsey joining her.

I couldn't listen to conspiracy theories while I was eating. I took my chances with my best friends.

I walked over to the table just in time to hear Kelsey say, "Did you see what Scarlet is wearing today?" She wrinkled her nose.

"Guh," Saylor said. "What's with her lately? The girl is slipping."

"Hi, Lavender," Zoe said in a too-nice voice.

"Hi," I said. I set my tray on the table and started to sit down.

"What do you think you're doing?" Zoe asked.

"Having lunch?" I answered. "You called me over."

Zoe, Kelsey, and Saylor laughed. "You thought you were going to have lunch with us?" Zoe said. "At *our* table?"

She was right. I hadn't been thinking clearly.

"Why did you wave me over then?" I asked.

They were still laughing. "I can't believe you actually thought we would want to sit with you! Like I could choke down food if your face was within my line of sight!"

Ha ha ha. Real funny. I wished Lavender were here to defend me. Although it's not like I'd done anything to help Lavender before when Zoe insulted her.

"We saw your name on the sign-up sheet for auditions today," Saylor said. "You're trying out for the lead?"

"That's right," I said.

They laughed. "So it's really true?" Kelsey said. "We thought it was a joke."

"Hate to break it to you, Lav, but you'll never get the lead," Zoe said. "You're just not lead material."

"You have to at least *look* like someone could fall in love with you," Kelsey said. They laughed again.

"We'll see," I said. But I was afraid they were right. Maybe auditioning was a big mistake. Lavender had been booed off the stage at the Talent Extravaganza. Why should the musical be any different?

I reached for my tray. "I'll be leaving then —"

"Where do you think you're going?" Zoe gripped my tray so I couldn't pick it up.

"But you just said —"

"I know what I said. I asked you over for a reason. And you don't know what it is yet."

"What is it?"

"Go buy me a Nutty Buddy."

"A what?"

"A Nutty Buddy." It was this ice-cream cone with nuts and chocolate on top. They sold it at the cafeteria.

"You don't like those," I said.

"Oooh," the other girls said.

"How do you know that?" Zoe practically yelled at me. "How do you, Lavender Schmitz, know what I like or don't like?"

Because I'm not Lavender! I felt like shouting. *I'm your best friend Scarlet and I know everything about you. Or at least I thought I did.*

"Just do as you're told," Kelsey said.

I couldn't believe Kelsey had just said that out loud. I'd never thought she was as bad as Zoe. But maybe she was.

I didn't have to take this from them. "Why should I?" I challenged.

Zoe picked up my chicken pot pie. I didn't normally like chicken pot pie, but Lavender's stomach was craving it.

"Because if you don't, your chicken pot pie is going down."

"All right, I'll go get you your stupid Nutty Buddy." I turned around to go back to the cafeteria line when I felt a *splotch!*

Something hit me in the back. I had a good idea what it was.

The whole cafeteria erupted in laughter. The chicken pot pie tin slid down my back and landed on the floor with a *clang*. I could feel the pie slime soaking through my shirt.

I turned around to face Zoe. "Why did you do that? I was getting your stupid Nutty Buddy."

"I didn't like your attitude," Zoe said. "Besides, I don't like Nutty Buddies."

"I know," I said through clenched teeth. "I told you that two minutes ago."

"You better go wash up," Kelsey said. "Need a clean shirt?" She threw something at me. I caught it. It was a T-shirt that said I CUT THE CHEESE AT THE BREAKWIND DINER.

"We saw it in the Lost and Found and knew it must be yours," Zoe said.

I tossed the T-shirt on the table and ran out of the room. Through my wet eyes everything blurred. The whole room was laughing and pointing at me. Even the Pimple Poppers.

I caught a glimpse of Charlie's face among the crowd. I almost didn't mind being humiliated in front of the whole school. Almost. But not in front of Charlie.

I ran to the nearest bathroom, but it was full of seventh graders and I didn't want them to see me crying. So I dashed into the music room, which was empty. I dove under a desk and curled up into a miserable little ball.

"Schmitzy?" The door opened and someone walked in. Great. More torture. Bring it on.

"Why don't you just leave me alone?" I cried.

I saw a pair of argyle kneesocks heading toward me. Maybelle's face peeked under the desk. "Schmitzy, are you okay?"

"No," I said. "Go away."

Maybelle didn't go away. She sat down with me under the desk.

"I saw what happened," she said. "I walked in right when they threw the pie at you. Why didn't you wait to have lunch with me?"

I hadn't thought of eating with Maybelle. I didn't know that was the plan. From now on I would.

"I don't know," I said. "I forgot."

"Why are you letting them get to you?" she said. "That's not like you. You're usually so good at ignoring them."

"I am?" *How could anybody do that?* I thought. *You'd have to be superhuman.*

"Yeah," Maybelle said. "It's one of the things I admire about you. You're like a duck. The rain rolls off your back."

"It's only because my back is so greasy. With chicken pot pie." I sniffled. "I guess they were just too mean for me today."

The door opened. We froze. A pair of sneakers, boy-sized, walked into the room and wandered around. Whoever it was seemed to be looking for something. We heard a boy's voice say, "There it is." The sneakers started for the door.

I sniffled again. I had to. I didn't have a tissue with me.

The sneakers stopped. Maybelle and I held our breath.

"Hey," the boy said. He knelt and peered under the desk. It was John Obrycki. "What are you guys doing under there?"

We crawled out. "What are *you* doing?" I asked. "Spying on us?" My brush with Zoe had left me a little touchy.

"I came to get my clarinet music," John said. "What's that goop all over your back?"

I almost started crying again.

"Zoe," Maybelle told him. John nodded. That was all he needed to hear.

"You need to borrow a shirt?" John said. "I've got a clean T-shirt in my locker. It's a little big for you, but —"

"It doesn't say anything embarrassing on it, does it?" I asked.

"Just CORY'S CABINS," John said. "Is that embarrassing? It's a campground my family goes to sometimes."

"That sounds fine," I said.

"I'll go get it." He left.

"What are you doing after school today?" Maybelle said. "Want to come over and make peanut butter brownies?"

"I'd like to," I said. "But I've got an audition today."

"You're auditioning for the musical?" Maybelle said. I braced myself for the backlash, but she was smiling. "That's fantastic! Why didn't you tell me?"

"I don't know," I said. Why wouldn't Lavender tell Maybelle about the auditions? Did she have a secret reason I didn't know about?

John returned, T-shirt in hand. Maybelle said, "John, Schmitzy's going to be in the musical."

"Well, I haven't tried out yet," I said.

"You'll get a good part for sure," John told me.

"You'll get the lead and Zoe will have to eat her words," Maybelle said. "Or else eat the chicken pot pie off your shirt."

"You'll show that whole stupid Glossy Posse," John said. "They should call them the Bossy Posse."

I laughed, and that spurred them to make even more silly jokes. It was weird — I was so used to making names for everyone else that it hadn't occurred to me that they'd have names for us. It almost made me feel better to know that.

When I went back to the bathroom this time, I wasn't crying. I changed into John's T-shirt. It was a little long, but it still felt like it fit.

I wasn't glossy and I'd lost my posse, but nothing would stop me from making it to that audition.

13

The Audition, Part 1

Ingrid Morganstern stood onstage singing "My White Knight" while Mr. Brummel accompanied her on the piano. It was the second day of auditions — M through Z — and Ingrid was trying out for Marian. She sang pretty well, but she was a big girl, taller than all of the boys. She'd be better as Eulalie Mackechnie Shinn, I thought. Eulalie Shinn was the mayor's pretentious wife.

I didn't want any competition for the part of Marian. Marian was meant for me and I was determined to get it. I didn't care if I had to play her in my body, Scarlet's body, or the corpse of Frankenstein's monster — I was going to get that part.

"Nice work, Ingrid," Mr. Brummel said when she stopped singing.

Ingrid beamed and walked off the stage. The auditorium was crowded. A lot of people were trying out, but others came just to watch. They laughed and jeered whenever someone onstage did something wrong — missed a line, sang off key, stumbled during a dance move. Mr. Brummel had to keep calling for quiet.

My heart was racing and my hands were clammy. I left the auditorium to perform Mr. Brummel's preaudition ritual. I slipped into the girls' room, checking under the stall doors to make sure no one was around. I had the bathroom to myself. I could begin.

I took a deep breath.

I whispered *Marian Marian Marian* backward, forward, upward, downward, inward, outward, eastward, westward, northward, and southward. And finally, heavenward.

"Please," I begged to the skies above. "I know it's a long shot. But it means so much to me. Please let me be Marian."

The bathroom was silent. I took another deep breath.

I felt silly. This would never work. How could a chant possibly make a wish come true?

But then, I thought as I brushed Scarlet's annoyingly long hair out of my face, if *this* could happen . . .

I didn't need to finish the thought.

How long was I going to be stuck in Scarlet's body? I had no idea. *Maybe I should throw the audition*, I thought. What if I did well today and Scarlet got the part, and then tomorrow I woke up as Lavender again and didn't get to play Marian?

On the other hand, what if I never went back to my old body again? If Scarlet got the part, I'd have the fun.

I didn't know what to do.

Something inside me said *Go for it.* Whatever happened, happened.

I was very nervous, of course. Terrified. But just two days in Scarlet's body had given me a boost of confidence. Even though I'd messed up the soccer game, I saw how people treated her differently from me. Maybe that would carry over into the audition. I wouldn't be awkward Lavender on that stage — I'd be graceful Scarlet. It had to help.

I went back into the auditorium. As I walked up the aisle toward the stage, Mr. Brummel announced, "Next up, Charlie Scott, auditioning for Professor Harold Hill."

Instead of taking a seat, I perched on the steps that led to the stage. From there I could see the faces in the audience.

Charlie took the stage, and the crowd grew quiet. He was a good singer and everybody knew it. Plus he had that *thing*. I didn't know what to call it, but he had this way about him that was extremely charming. I once heard of a whistle only dogs could hear. Charlie's charisma was like a whistle only girls could hear.

Mr. Brummel nodded at him from the piano. "I'll be singing 'Marian the Librarian,' " Charlie said.

I melted. "Marian the Librarian" was a melty song. In the musical, Harold Hill, a con man, was trying to convince cold-hearted Marian to trust him. I had the original cast sound track recording of *The Music Man*, both the Broadway version and the movie version (on vinyl, of course), and I'd listened to them about a thousand times. "Marian" was the song I wished a boy would sing to me, if only my name was Marian . . . and I knew a boy I could stand to be around.

Mr. Brummel played the intro. Charlie brushed the hair out of his face, took a breath, and sang. Suddenly he wasn't a gawky eighth-grade boy anymore. He turned into a suave young man, singing to Marian. Calling to her. Melting her.

From my perch on the stage steps, I watched the audience. Most of the boys fidgeted and twitched as if they wished they could change the channel. But the girls, almost all of them, were in a trance. Scarlet most of all. The look on her face — *my* face — transformed it. She glowed.

I liked Charlie, but it was the song that got to me. From the look on Scarlet's face, though, Charlie's singing — or maybe Charlie himself — was the magic for her.

Charlie finished the song, and the audience cheered. He smiled, slid the curtain of hair back over his face, blushed as boyishly as possible, and hurried off the stage.

"Very nice, Charlie." Mr. Brummel said the same thing to everybody, but he was obviously impressed. "Scarlet Martinez. You're next."

I got to my feet and walked to the center of the stage. "I'm trying out for Marian," I said. "I'll be singing 'Goodnight, My Someone.'"

"Goodnight, My Someone" was a sweet lullaby sung by a lonely woman — Marian — who knew her true love was out there somewhere. She just hadn't found him yet. I'd sung this song a thousand times — in my bedroom, in the shower, while riding my bike. I knew it cold.

But my hands grew clammy, right on cue. I felt a few beads of sweat break out on my forehead. Everyone was staring at me.

I'm going to mess it up, I thought.

I cleared my throat and looked at the faces. The audience was respectfully quiet, because they thought I was Scarlet the Popular Girl. *Calm down*, I told myself. *This will be easy.*

I opened my mouth to sing, and it all fell apart.

The words croaked out of me. I sang all the wrong notes. My voice sounded like a dentist's drill set on *Screeeeeeeeeeeeech*.

The crowd shifted restlessly, but they didn't boo or jeer the way they would have if they'd known that I, *Lavender*, was singing. Kelsey and Zoe sat in the back row, smirking.

They'd tried to warn me. They knew something was wrong with my plan to star in the musical. I should have guessed.

Scarlet was tone deaf. To call her voice froggy was an insult to amphibians.

But I was stuck onstage in the middle of the song. It was my duty to finish. Stopping in the middle and running away in shame would only make things worse.

So I croaked out the rest of the song. It was so bad I wanted to cover my own ears.

Scarlet crouched in the front row, head in her hands, embarrassed. *That* look I recognized. No more glow.

She could have warned me.

At last the torture ended. There was a smattering of polite applause. Red-faced, I hurried off the stage before Mr. Brummel could say "Very nice, Scarlet" with total insincerity.

I raced down the aisle, feeling everyone's eyes on me. I just wanted to get out of there, but Zoe and Kelsey blocked the door.

"What were you thinking?" Zoe asked. "Singing like that in front of everybody?"

"Are you trying to geek yourself up on purpose?" Kelsey said.

"Are you *looking* for humiliation?"

At that moment all I could think was, *I miss Maybelle.*

"Thanks for your support," I said. I tried to push past them, but they weren't finished yet.

"You're lucky we're your friends," Zoe told me. "We'll tell everyone you were up there for a joke. Making fun of the musical, and how dorky it is. They'll believe us. They'll think it's *hysterical.*"

"You sure proved how dorky it was," Kelsey said.

I couldn't let that go unanswered. "Shut your mouth," I told her. "The musical is *not* dorky."

"What?" Kelsey looked shocked. "Did you just tell me to shut my mouth?"

"You'd better be nice to us, Scarlet," Zoe said. "You need us. Without us, you don't have anyone."

Was that really true? Scarlet didn't have any real friends except for them?

"So what," I said. "I don't need anyone."

"Oh really?" Zoe threatened. "You'll see."

"Really," I told her.

Bring it on.

14

The Audition, Part 2

I rubbed my sweaty hands on my pants, waiting for my turn. My stomach clenched. I was glad that chicken pot pie had never made it into my mouth. What was the one thing worse than ruining an audition? Ruining an audition by ralphing onstage.

At first I thought Lavender was messing up on purpose — making me sound bad because she didn't want "Scarlet" to get the lead.

But she wouldn't do that. If she was stuck in my body, she'd want to play Marian. And her voice was so terrible it couldn't be faked.

Then I remembered that it wasn't her voice making that terrible screeching noise. It was *my* voice.

I cringed. Did I really sound like that? Why hadn't anyone ever told me I couldn't sing?

The worst part was that Charlie was still in the auditorium, watching. I remembered the nice things he'd said about me, how pretty I was, how good I'd be as Marian. Now that he'd heard me sing, would he still want to share a stage with me? Not as Scarlet, not with that voice.

Lavender slinked off the stage, humiliated. For a second I was grateful she was the one who had to endure the embarrassment and not me.

But everyone thought *I* was the one who'd messed up. When word of "my" terrible audition got out, the whole school would know I'd made a complete fool out of myself.

And now it was my turn — in Lavender's body. My turn to make a total fool of myself all over again.

"Lavender Schmitz," Mr. Brummel called.

I mounted the stairs to the stage. I caught a glimpse of Charlie in the audience. His audition had been so amazing I forgot where I was. Seriously. If you had asked me what planet I was on while he was singing, I would have guessed Pluto. His voice was like gold, like chocolate, like rose petals. Sweet as the arc of a perfect penalty kick that goes straight into the goal. And he was singing to me, me alone. I felt convinced of it.

Mr. Brummel knocked me back down to reality. "Okay, Lavender, what will it be today?"

" 'Shipoopi'!" somebody yelled.

I'd listened to "Shipoopi" in Lavender's room the night before. It was a funny song sung by a short, fat man. "Shipoopi" was not a good thing to yell at a girl trying out for Marian.

"I'm going to sing 'Till There Was You,' " I said.

"So you're auditioning for Marian?" Mr. Brummel said.

"Yes," I said. A laugh rippled through the crowd.

Mr. Brummel played the intro. I took a deep breath and opened my mouth to sing. My brain emptied. I closed my mouth.

I'd forgotten the words.

I'd practiced the song over and over again the night before. I must have listened to Lavender's *Music Man* record twenty times. Lavender's father had said that if he heard the record one more time, he'd personally break it into nacho-sized pieces, melt cheese on them in the microwave, and eat them with salsa. I figured he was kidding, but I couldn't be sure, so I put on Lavender's headphones and practiced the song some more until I knew it cold.

But up on the stage my mind went blank.

Mr. Brummel stopped. "Are you ready, Lavender?"

"Yes, I —"

"Psst! Lavender! Here!"

Charlie reached out and pushed a lyric sheet into my hand.

"Thank you," I said. Charlie nodded and sat down. I smiled at him. My hero.

I glanced at the lyrics. From the first words, the song came flooding back to me.

I nodded at Mr. Brummel. I was ready.

He replayed the introduction, and I started to sing, quietly. My voice quavered.

"Sing out, Lavender," Mr. Brummel said. "You can do it."

I sang out louder. And even louder. My voice was strong. And it sounded good. Really good.

I could sing!

It was a wonderful feeling, like gliding through water. Like flying. I'd never realized that Lavender had this power inside of her. Why hadn't she used it?

People had teased me about my singing before, but I'd thought they were teasing me because they liked to tease. I knew I was no Adele, but I'd thought my singing was okay.

Now I understood. I couldn't sing before, not at all. I didn't know what it felt like to *really* sing, with a powerful, clear voice.

Maybe Lavender didn't want to let anyone see how talented she was, but that wasn't my style. If I had a voice like this, I'd use it. I'd love it! And for now, I *did* have this beautiful voice. I refused to hide it. I let it soar out over the auditorium.

When the song was over, Mr. Brummel smiled. The audience was sort of quiet. Nobody booed or anything.

"Lovely, Lavender," Mr. Brummel said. I walked off the stage, down the aisle toward the back door, where Maybelle waited for me.

Charlie reached out from his seat and touched my arm.

"That was really good," he said.

"Thanks," I said. Charlie turned his attention back to the stage and the next audition. My arm warmed where he had touched it.

"Lavender, you were fantastic!" Maybelle whispered. We went out into the lobby. "I always knew you were a good singer but that was the best I've ever heard you!"

"Thank you." My body shook from the rush of excitement. "Do you think I have a chance at the part?"

"Definitely," Maybelle said. "Mr. Brummel would be crazy not to give it to you."

Another rush shot through me.

What if I really did it — won the starring role? Opposite Charlie Scott! Endless hours of rehearsal. A kissing scene! Which we'd have to practice a lot. Over and over and over.

I had a good chance. I could feel it.

As long as I had Lavender's voice. And that meant staying in Lavender's body.

"Woo-hoo!" I yelled. I jumped up and landed on the outside of my left foot.

"Careful, Schmitzy," Maybelle said. "You don't want to twist your ankle right before rehearsals begin."

"What are you so hyped up about?" Kelsey asked. If I'd known Zoe and Kelsey were lurking in the lobby, I wouldn't have woo-hoo'd.

"You think you're going to get the lead?" Zoe said. "Don't get your hopes up."

"Lavender has a great chance," Maybelle said. "She's a better singer than anybody in that room."

"So what?" Zoe said. "She still looks like a cavegirl. It's *The Music Man*, not *Planet of the Apes*."

"She looks beautiful when she sings," Maybelle said. "The music transforms her."

Zoe and Kelsey snickered. Even I thought that was a bit of a stretch. But I knew what Maybelle meant. I *felt* transformed when I was singing. I felt like a star.

"You might get a part, but you'll never get the lead," Zoe said. "I'm doing you a favor, telling you this. So you won't be disappointed."

"Even Scarlet has a better shot than you, and she's terrible," Kelsey said.

That hurt. It hurt when they insulted Lavender, and it hurt when they insulted me. If they'd insulted Maybelle, that would have hurt too.

"You're in for a shock, Zoe," I said. "Guess what: The casting isn't up to you. Come on, Maybelle."

Maybelle and I walked away. Behind us, Zoe and Kelsey whispered and laughed. I knew better than to look back. It would only spur them on.

But my confidence faded. What if they were right? I was Lavender now. Maybe I could sing. But I didn't have the luck. I didn't have the grace, the charisma that a leading lady needed. I had the Lavender Curse.

"Don't listen to them." Maybelle stopped at the bike rack and unlocked her bike. "You're going to get the lead, Schmitzy. I feel it in my bones." She hopped on her bike. "See you tomorrow, first thing. I'm telling you, your name is going to be on that list!" She rode away.

"Scarlet!" Lavender called to me from the auditorium. I waited for her to catch up.

"Nice job," she said. "I hope you're enjoying *my* voice. Yours turned out to be a dud."

"Sorry," I said. "I never realized what a bad singer I am."

"I guess things always sound better in the shower," Lavender said. "Have you come up with any brilliant ideas about how we could get our real bodies back? I'm getting a little itchy in here."

"No," I said. "Have you?"

"If I do, you'll be the first to hear about it."

"Same here," I said. We both sighed. There was nothing to do but wait for Mr. Brummel to post the cast list in the morning.

"Tell my parents how well the audition went," Lavender said. "They'll be happy."

"I will," I said.

"I wish I could see their faces," Lavender said.

To my surprise, I wished she could too.

To celebrate the audition, Lavender's mother took me shopping on 36th Street. She couldn't believe it when I agreed to go. She was thrilled. But I loved shopping, and Lavender definitely needed some new clothes. The hard part was keeping her mother from suspecting that

Lavender was no longer Lavender. She kept looking at me like I had two heads.

We went to all the cute little boutiques. Finding clothes for Lavender's short, stocky body was not easy. The salesgirls would say, "Oh, that looks great on you" about stuff that *didn't* look great, in this condescending voice. Like they'd all laugh about it later over smoothies.

I ignored them, picking out a new pair of jeans and a cute top to go with it. At Maroc I went straight for the best pair of boots, but when I looked at the price tag I wondered if Lavender's parents could afford them. My mom would have bought them without a thought, but I knew Lavender's family didn't have as much money as we did, so I put them back. There was a thrift store down the street, where I found a pretty blue sweater and a great pair of platform sandals in Lavender's size that cost a lot less.

"What about contact lenses?" I asked Lavender's mother. I was tired of wearing Lavender's clunky glasses and thought she'd look better without them. "Are they too expensive?"

"If you need contacts, we'll find a way to pay for them." Lavender's mother could hardly contain her excitement. "What's gotten into you, Lavender? I'm almost afraid to ask. I don't want to jinx it."

"Maybe it's better you don't ask, then," I said. That answer seemed to satisfy her. It sounded like something Lavender would say.

It was fun shopping with Lavender's mom. She was so proud of me, so eager to make me happy. We tried on funny hats and glasses; we laughed and joked. When I went shopping with my own mother, she didn't like most of the clothes I picked out and criticized the way I looked in everything. Shopping with her wasn't fun. It was a job. I felt sad thinking about it.

When we got home, Mrs. Schmitz preceded me into the kitchen and said, "Ta-da!"

Mr. Schmitz gawked at me. "Who's this? Miss America?"

"Stop it," I said. "They're just clothes."

Rosemary said, "Are you going to start acting all teenagery now that you're thirteen?"

"Yes, I am, little punk," I said. "So get used to it. You can learn from watching me so you don't turn out all dorky like your sister."

Rosemary looked at me funny, blinking her big blue eyes behind her glasses, and I realized what I'd just said.

"I mean, like I used to be," I said. "Until I turned thirteen."

"Don't change too much, Lavender," Rosemary said. "I like the old, dorky you too."

"Dorkiness is our heritage," Mr. Schmitz said. "Passed on from father to son and mother to daughter for generations of Schmitzes."

"What are you trying to do, curse me for life?" Sometimes I couldn't believe this family. They actually prized being awkward and clunky. Like they thought it was a good thing, just because that was how they'd always been, and it could never change.

"Someday you'll realize that being a Schmitz is not a curse, Lavender," her father said. "It's just who you are."

"I don't see the difference," I said.

But maybe I was starting to.

15

The Cast List

"All hail Her Highness, Princess Plastic." Ben bowed low before me, sweeping the floor with his hand, as I passed him on the way to dinner.

I was not in the mood for this. "You *should* bow before me," I said. "I deserve it. Because I'm the best ally you've got in this family."

Ben lifted his head in surprise. That was not the kind of answer he usually got from Scarlet.

"Be nice to Scarlet tonight," Scarlet's mom said to Ben as we walked into the dining room. "She's had a rough day."

How did she know that? I hadn't told her anything about the auditions. As soon as I'd gotten home from school I'd gone straight to Scarlet's room and shut the door. I guessed the pain showed on my face.

But it wasn't the pain that had tipped her off.

"No makeup, baggy sweats on, and looks like she hasn't brushed her hair all day," she said. "I know my daughter, and that spells trouble."

I touched my tangled hair. "My hair does not spell anything. It's *artfully tousled.*"

I'd seen that phrase in one of Scarlet's *Seventeen* maga-
zines. I'd flipped through a few of them that afternoon, trying
to forget the pain of the audition.

Steve glanced up from reading messages on his phone to
check on my hair. "Just looks messy to me. Put your game
away and sit down, Ben. It's time to eat."

Ben raised his empty hands — he wasn't playing a
game — and sat down at the table. "You're the one who's fid-
dling with his phone."

Steve typed a few characters and didn't look up this time.
"That's different — this is important."

"Whatever," Ben said. "But I wasn't playing a game. If you
looked up from your phone for two seconds, you would have
seen that."

Now Steve put his phone in his pocket and lifted his head.
"We're going to have a nice family dinner now — right, Leigh?
Right."

"Oh! Right." Scarlet's mom set a large plastic platter of
roast chicken on the table. "Who wants rice?"

Steve watched her. "Did you do something to your hair? It
looks blonder."

She touched her newly dyed hair nervously. "Yes. Do you
like it?"

"Don't let it get too light. It's starting to get a radioac-
tive glow."

She laughed a kind of fakey laugh, but I wasn't sure Steve
was joking.

We ate takeout chicken — Scarlet's family must have

spent a fortune on takeout. Even the fancy dinner with the Mortensons had been bought at a gourmet catering shop. They had this big, shiny kitchen but they didn't use it for much more than microwaving leftovers.

"How was your soccer game, Scarlet?" Scarlet's mom asked.

"That was yesterday," I said.

"She auditioned for the school musical today," Ben chimed in. I was glad *someone* was paying attention.

"Oh." Scarlet's mom picked at a chicken breast. "How did it go?"

"How do you *think* it went?" I was still feeling very crabby about it.

"I'm guessing not so great," Steve said. "Correct?"

"Correct."

"Can you sing? I don't think I've ever heard you sing," Steve said.

"I thought I could, but I was wrong."

Steve chuckled. "So I guess you learned your lesson, huh? Stick to what you know you're good at. It's not worth putting yourself out on a limb — you'll only embarrass yourself."

"Steve's right, honey," Scarlet's mom said. "There's nothing worse than making a fool of yourself."

"Do you really believe that?" I asked. If making a fool of yourself was the worst thing in the world, then I had to be the lowest human in the history of mankind. I'd been embarrassed almost every day of my thirteen years. Did that make me a bad person?

"Take that time Ben liked that girl in his class," Steve said. "What was her name? Ina?"

"Ida." Ben began to slump in his chair.

"Ida. Pretty girl. You had just gotten your braces then, and you had that skin problem —"

"Dad." Ben was sinking lower. His head was about level with mine at this point.

"So you had the brilliant idea of writing a poem for her and asking her to a dance. I told you poetry was not your strong suit, but you didn't listen —"

"Please, Dad."

As much as I wanted to hear this story of Ben's humiliation by a girl, I also began to get the queasy feeling that his father was embarrassing him all over again, and getting a kick out of it. Which made the story hard to enjoy.

Steve would not let up. "I can still remember some of the choicer lines." He started chuckling, and then lifted one hand in dramatic-poet fashion and recited:

"You're greater than Star Wars: Episode Three,

Known as Revenge of the Sith.

I would be so very hap-pee

If you to the dance

Me would go with."

I wanted to laugh. I really did. Because it was hands down the worst poem I'd ever heard. Also, if he was trying to do

Yoda talk, he got it wrong. But Ben looked so embarrassed and miserable that the laugh died in my throat.

Steve pressed on. "Do you remember what Ida said after you read the poem to her in front of your whole eighth-grade class?"

"No," Ben said. "But I bet you do."

"Come on, Ben. You remember. You sulked about it for days."

Ben didn't answer. He had drifted so far down in his chair that his chin was almost level with the table.

"I think we can all guess what Ida said," I cut in. "Why do you have to be so mean about it?"

The table went silent. The three of them stared at me, stunned.

"I'm not being mean," Steve said. "I'm trying to teach Ben — and you — a valuable lesson about dignity."

"By embarrassing us? How does that teach us dignity?"

Scarlet's mom looked like a deer facing a hunter's rifle. "Scarlet, what's gotten into you?"

A little bit of Lavender, I thought. "I think any boy who writes a poem for a girl and reads it out loud to the whole class is pretty brave. Even if the poem happened to be about *Star Wars*."

"Scarlet, you don't speak to me that way," Steve said. "Go to your room and stay there. You're going to have to skip dinner tonight."

"No, I won't," I said. "I'm a growing girl and I'm hungry after a long hard day at school. I'll go to my room, all right, but

I'm taking my dinner with me." I loaded my plate with extra chicken and rice.

I turned to Ben, but he wasn't sitting up any straighter in his seat. He still looked miserable and embarrassed and not grateful that I'd defended him at all.

I tried to send him a psychic message: *Ben, we're in this together.* Or at least he and Scarlet were. They might as well team up and support each other.

But I don't think he got the message.

I took my plate up to Scarlet's room, where I could eat in peace.

Now that I was alone, memories of my painful audition washed over me. Was it possible that Steve was right? I *had* made a fool of myself in front of the whole school. I'd lost my dream part. Marian. All because I was stuck in this body I never asked for.

But then I looked around at Scarlet's luxurious room, a monument to good luck and success. A charmed life. Her soccer trophies, lined up on a shelf. The grinning pictures of her with all her friends. The birthday gifts, still piled on her dresser. Charlie's blue flowers, wilting in a vase. This was the bedroom of a girl who had everything. A girl who got what she wanted.

What was I so worried about? I was *Scarlet Martinez.*

I pinned my hair up in a bun and stared at myself in the mirror. I looked prim and pretty, the perfect Marian the Librarian.

Maybe that would be enough. A few of the other girls at the audition were good singers, but none of them were mind-blowingly good except . . . me. Or rather, Scarlet. With my former vocal cords.

But that old me was *Lavender Schmitz*. She didn't look anything like pretty blond Shirley Jones, who played Marian in the movie. Lavender didn't look like someone Charlie Scott would glance twice at, much less fall in love with.

Maybe there was hope. Maybe, as Scarlet, I'd still get the part. So what if I couldn't sing? Maybe I could lip-synch! I could act the part of Marian while Scarlet, in my body, stood behind the curtain and sang the songs for me, just like Debbie Reynolds in *Singin' in the Rain*. If only I'd suggested it to Mr. Brummel earlier . . .

There was still a chance. If Mr. Brummel could overlook my voice, he might give me the lead anyway.

Stranger things had happened.

The next morning I woke up before my alarm went off. I threw on some Scarlet clothes and hurried out of the house without stopping for breakfast.

It was a cool, sunny fall day. The leaves on the trees were just turning orange. I marched through Scarlet's neighborhood chanting *Marian, Marian, Marian*. The big old houses, winding, hilly roads, and leafy yards were so different from my own neighborhood. My street, lined with brick row houses crammed together on tiny plots, seemed shabby compared to this. But I still loved it.

I stopped on the hill above Falls Road. Below me, the kids marched into school like ants, one line coming from Roland Park, the other from Hampden. They filed into the giant ant farm that was our school and disappeared, ready for another day of battle.

Marian, Marian, Marian.

I ran down the hill and followed them inside, heading straight for the bulletin board outside the music room. A crowd buzzed around it. The list had been posted.

"Let me see! Let me see!" I elbowed my way through the crowd. Luckily, with Scarlet's height, I could see over most people's heads.

Cast list for The Music Man

Professor Harold Hill............................Charlie Scott
Marian Paroo............................Lavender Schmitz

Lavender Schmitz! That was me!

I stopped, blinked, and read the list again. There it was, in black and white: my name, Lavender Schmitz.

I got the part! I was going to play Marian!

"Why are you screaming?" Kelsey asked me. She and Zoe had joined the throng struggling to read the list. "Being in the chorus isn't *that* exciting."

Being in the what?

I came to my senses. I wasn't Lavender Schmitz. I was Scarlet Martinez. I skimmed the list until I found her name, bunched up with the rest of the rejects in the chorus.

I knew for a fact that Mr. Brummel didn't turn anyone away for the chorus. If they couldn't sing, they got a dancing part. That was what I was destined for: A dancing part in the chorus.

Not *Marian Marian Marian*.

Mr. Brummel's old good-luck superstition hadn't worked after all.

"Holy guacamole! Lavender!" Maybelle jumped up to see over the heads of the crowd. "Lavender!" she shouted. "You're Marian!"

"What?" Scarlet's face lit up.

Maybelle hugged her. Scarlet looked stunned, but happy. She hugged Maybelle back. They jumped up and down, the way Scarlet used to do with Zoe and Kelsey. "I don't believe it! I don't believe it!"

"*I* don't believe it either," Zoe said. "That troll opposite Charlie Scott? Did they change the musical to *Beauty and the Beast*?"

"The play's going to stink," Kelsey said. "Charlie kissing Lavender? Who wants to see *that*?"

"Even *you* would have been better than Lavender, Scarlet," Zoe said.

I drifted away, fuming. I didn't want to talk to anyone.

My best friend, Maybelle, was unwittingly cheering on Scarlet. And Scarlet's so-called friends were no help at all.

Scarlet was even more charmed than I thought. Even when she was stuck in my old, klutzy body, she still won. She still got the part, got to be with the boy she liked, got everything!

But she got the lead using *my* voice. That was what killed me. It was my voice! I'd worked on those songs. I'd practiced them and loved them. She hadn't even known them until two days ago. She'd learned them from *my* records. Which she found in *my* room!

That part was mine. I deserved it.

"Scarlet?" Kelsey said. "You're not really bumming about the cast list, are you? The very fact that Lavender got the lead shows what a waste the musical is. Why bother with it?"

"She *is* upset," Zoe said. "I can see it in her face. By the way, is the electricity out at your house? You look like you got dressed in the dark."

I glanced down at my clothes. A purple sweater over red plaid pants and green sneakers. Clashy, and not in a good way. I still hadn't bothered to brush my hair. And I wouldn't have known how to put on Scarlet's makeup if I'd wanted to.

I'd kind of hoped I couldn't go wrong with anything in Scarlet's closet. She didn't own anything that wasn't fashionable.

But you could put her clothes together in a cool way, or you could put them together in a pathetic way. Which, according to Zoe, was exactly what I had done.

"You better get it together, Scarlet," Zoe said in this whispery way that made it seem as if she was trying to help me. "You've lost your touch. I'm — I'm a little embarrassed to be seen with you. I'm telling you this as a friend."

"Embarrassed to be seen with me?" I said. "What do you mean?" *I'm Scarlet Martinez*, I thought. *I am not embarrassing.*

But evidently I *was* embarrassing. My natural geekiness was leaking out, transforming Scarlet from hotsy to notsy. Like a balloon with a tiny hole in it, slowly losing air until it's nothing but a wrinkly piece of rubber. Scarlet had sprung a geek-leak.

"Let's just say your social rating is way down," Zoe said. "I heard the jock boys talking at lunch the other day. You used to be a 9.7. You're down to eight and slipping."

"So? What do I care what a bunch of stupid jocks think?" I said.

Zoe shrugged. "It's not my problem. But if your social stock falls, you lose power."

"What power?" I said. "The power to keep people from picking on me, the way they pick on Lavender?"

"That's one way of putting it," Zoe said.

I'd end up where I started — Lavender with a different name. Pariah of the school.

Because that was who I really was on the inside. And no matter whose body I wore on the outside, I couldn't escape myself.

16

A Whole New Lavender

"Congratulations, Lavender." Charlie shook my hand. "I'm glad you got the part. You really sold that song in your audition."

"Thank you." My heart bounced around my rib cage. The voice that won the lead may have been Lavender's, but the actress part was me. When Lavender was onstage she kind of flinched, as if she expected to be booed.

"So you're a triple threat," Charlie said. "You sing, you act, you play the ukulele."

"I don't play the ukulele," I said.

"Yes you do," Charlie said. "I saw you play at the Talent Extravaganza."

Oh. Right.

"Unless you uke-synched it," he said.

"Oh. No, that performance was all too real." I remembered how the audience had booed Lavender. No wonder she flinched when she went onstage.

I would have never booed her. If only I'd known.

"You were good," Charlie said.

"I'm thinking of switching to guitar," I said. "Much

cooler. Meanwhile . . . I guess we'll be spending a lot of time together now. Working on the musical, I mean."

"Yeah." He dug the heel of his sneaker into the floor tile. "Maybe you can come over to my house after school sometime. To practice our lines and stuff."

"Awesome," I said. "I'm going to need a lot of practice."

"No, you won't," Charlie said. "You're a natural."

"Yes, I will," I said. "Trust me."

It might not be so terrible, being Lavender, I thought. Just for a little while.

"You look great today, Schmitzy," Maybelle said to me. We were walking down the hall together after English. "There's something different about you."

If only you knew, I thought. "No more glasses," I said.

"Of course!" Maybelle said. "I can't believe I didn't notice right away. I guess the Marian news side-tracked me!"

"And I thought I'd wash my hair for once," I added.

"Whoa," Maybelle said. "Don't change too much, or I won't recognize you."

"Ha ha."

I kept an eye out for Lavender — to avoid her. I felt guilty about the audition, and I was afraid of what she'd do when she saw the makeover I'd given her. Lavender's hair wasn't half-bad, once I washed it and brushed it about a thousand times. It was thick, I had to give it that. I'd found a few old barrettes in the dust under Lavender's dresser, washed them off, and stuck them in her hair to keep it under control.

"So guess what?" Maybelle said. "I have a feeling Ian Colburn is going to ask me to the Halloween Spooktacular!"

"Really?" I said, but what I thought was *Uh-oh*. Zoe had been eyeing Ian all year. And what Zoe wanted, Zoe got. If not, someone had to pay. I didn't want that someone to be Maybelle.

"What makes you think he's going to ask you?" I hedged.

"Someone left this note taped to my locker." Maybelle handed me a folded piece of paper. It said:

DO YOU HAVE A DATE FOR THE SPOOKTACULAR YET?
CHECK THE APROPREATE BOX: ___YES ___NO
LEAVE THIS NOTE TAPED TO YOUR LOCKER. I LL PICK
IT UP LATER, IN SECRIT.
SINED,
A YELLOW-BELLIED ADMIROR

Maybelle had checked *no*.

"A yellow-bellied admirer?" I said. "Why do you think it's Ian?"

"Because he's a terrible speller," Maybelle said. "The spelling gives him away."

I was worried. What if Maybelle was being set up for a prank? What if Zoe had seen Ian talking to Maybelle, got jealous, and decided to do something mean — like fake a note from Ian? Maybe the bad spelling had been done on purpose to make Maybelle *think* the note was from Ian.

Listen to yourself, I thought. *This is the way Zoe makes you think.*

"Be careful, Maybelle," I said. "Don't get your hopes up too high."

"You're right," Maybelle said. "I don't know *for sure* who the note is from. But I really think it's from Ian."

I shook my head sadly. Maybelle was so sweet, she couldn't even imagine the mean things a mind like Zoe's could cook up.

"Are you going to the Spooktacular, Schmitzy?" Maybelle asked. "You don't have to have a date, you know."

"I know."

"Maybe Charlie will ask you."

"Charlie? Do you really think so?"

"I think he's starting to like you," Maybelle said.

"I kind of thought he liked Scarlet."

"I used to think so too. But I'm beginning to change my mind. The way you sang at the audition . . . well, I think a lot of people see you in a new way now."

Aha. There was a good reason for that. *I* was Lavender now. People could sense the difference. They didn't know why. All they knew was suddenly Lavender was getting less odd and more . . . normal.

The bell rang. I had art; Maybelle had algebra. "See you at lunch?" I asked.

"See you at lunch."

"Good." I looked forward to having lunch with her. I would have liked to have lunch with her every day.

I sat in the art room, wondering what to do with the hideous acrylic painting Lavender was working on. She was even worse at art than I was. The paper was smeared with strips of green and black paint. I couldn't tell what it was supposed to be.

John Obrycki sat next to me. He was wearing a smock. "How's the sunset coming?" he asked.

"Sunset?" What kind of sunset was green and black?

"Isn't this the picture you were telling me about last week?" he said. "The Toxic Sunset?"

"Oh. The *Toxic* Sunset. Right." The toxic part was right; I still wasn't sure about the sunset.

"I'd temper these greens with some blues and yellows," John told me. "And go easy on the black."

"Thanks." That gave me somewhere to start. I grabbed a bottle of yellow paint and a bottle of blue and tried to make the smudge look more like a sunset.

Last year John had won a blue ribbon at the middle school art show. I remembered because the drawing he did — a portrait of his dog — was so good. And he'd made that origami star for Lavender's birthday. It was still sitting on the top shelf in Lavender's locker.

"Congratulations on the play," John said while he effortlessly molded a piece of clay into a dog's head. "I saw the auditions. You were the best by far."

"Thanks," I said.

He looked at me as if he was expecting me to add something else.

"Um, it was nice of you to come watch me."

He still stared at me in that odd way, like he was waiting for a blow to the head.

"Aren't you going to make some kind of mean comment about how I should have had better things to do, or how you appreciate my interest in your public embarrassment?" he asked.

"No," I said. "Why would I do that?"

"That's the kind of thing you normally say to me."

"It is?" Duh, of course it was. I kept forgetting how good Lavender was at losing friends and alienating people.

I racked my brain for something snarky to say, to keep the Lavender illusion going. But I couldn't come up with anything. I wasn't good at witty comebacks, nasty or nice.

Why should I be sarcastic anyway? Just because she was? I liked her friends. They were actually nice to me.

"I'm sorry," I said. "From now on I'll try not to make snarky remarks."

"That's okay," John said. "I kind of like your snarky remarks. Although not when you, like, put yourself down."

"Oh."

He went back to his dog's head, and I kept on brightening up the Toxic Sunset.

I'd thought Lavender loved being a weirdo and an outsider. But what did I know?

I was only certain of one thing. Now that she — meaning I — had the lead in the school musical, all that could change. *Would* change.

The world was about to meet a whole new Lavender.

17

Secret Password

I hadn't seen Scarlet all morning. I looked for her every time I passed through the halls. Where was she? Madame Geller was calling on me a lot in French and getting suspicious when I started coughing uncontrollably every single time. (She said something in French which I didn't understand but had a feeling meant, *Scarlet, I'm onto you.*) I needed Scarlet to tell me at least one phrase I could use to put her off — something that meant, *It's on the tip of my tongue.*

I knew Scarlet would be in the art room, so I managed to escape study hall a few minutes early and creep up to the third floor where the studio was. The door was open so I peeked inside. Mr. Booth, the art teacher, was carving a soap sculpture at his desk, not paying any attention. Everyone else was quietly working on projects.

I hope Scarlet's not ruining my painting, I thought, scanning the room. *It's bad enough she stole the part that's rightfully mine.*

There she was, sitting in the corner with my painting in front of her — daubing *yellow* onto it!

Wait — *was* that her? She looked very different from my usual Lavender self.

She'd brushed my hair and pinned it back with barrettes. She'd dressed my body in new clothes I'd never seen before. Jeans! And platform shoes! I would never be caught dead dressed like that!

And *WHERE WERE MY GLASSES?!?*

Scarlet had a lot of nerve. She was taking over my life!

Then I noticed something even worse. She was sitting at a table with John Obrycki, and they were talking and laughing like they were having a good time. Like they liked each other. Like they *like*-liked each other.

John took a scrap of paper and folded it into a bird. He moved the bird's mouth and made it talk. Scarlet giggled.

What was he saying to her?

Wait a second. Were John and Scarlet . . . *flirting*?

I felt a twinge of jealousy. Which surprised me. Because I didn't like John Obrycki. I mean, I *liked* him, but I didn't like him *like that*. I didn't have anything against him. But he was a boy, and I was not the boy-crazy type.

Then I wondered: How come he never flirted with me when *I* was Lavender?

I couldn't hear what they were saying, but I was seized with a terrible need to find out. The bell rang. I was supposed to go to gym while they had lunch.

Kids started pouring out of the art room. I ducked behind the door. John and Scarlet left together, still talking, barely noticing anything around them. It would be easy to follow them without being detected. So I did. I'd just have to be a little late for gym.

I couldn't get over what Scarlet had done to me. She had dressed my body in the kind of clothes *she* would wear. Who did she think she was? She may have been inhabiting my body, but she was *not* me.

I was so busy watching Scarlet and John joke and laugh like old buddies that I almost crashed into Kelsey and Zoe.

"Where are you going, Scar?" Zoe asked. "You've got gym now, don't you?"

"What? Oh yeah."

Kelsey noticed that my eyes were glued to Scarlet and John. "Did you see that?" she asked. "Lavender actually brushed her hair this morning! And she wore decent clothes for once." She glanced back at my old body, which was disappearing down the hall with John. I tried to push past Zoe and Kelsey, but they pulled me in the other direction.

"It's pathetic," Zoe said. "She'll never be pretty. Why bother trying?"

"I don't know," Kelsey said. "I think she looks pretty good. A lot better, anyway."

"Shush." Zoe elbowed Kelsey, who backtracked.

"Um, well, of course, *anything* would be better than how she used to look."

Some kids I barely knew stopped Scarlet to congratulate her about the musical. Kelsey and Zoe blabbed on and on, but I hardly listened. The interesting stuff was happening to another Lavender.

It was like watching a movie about myself. With an actress playing the part of me. Only the story had been changed from gloomy to happy. And the actress played Lavender so that I hardly recognized her.

I wanted to jump up and down and yell, "John, that girl is an imposter! *I'm* the real Lavender!"

But of course I couldn't. That would look crazy.

My confusion fell away and it all became clear to me. I knew exactly what I wanted. I wanted to play Marian. And I wanted to go to the Spooktacular with John.

How could I stand by in this good-looking, tone-deaf body and watch while Scarlet experienced the most glorious moments of my entire life?

I couldn't.

I had to do something right away. But I didn't know what. I was stuck.

Also, I had gym. Which made me wish I were literally stuck, just for an hour, so I could get out of it.

How dare she interfere with my life? I muttered while the gym teacher made us do sprints up and down the bleachers. Which, I found, were a lot easier if your body was in shape, as Scarlet's was. In my own body I wouldn't have had enough breath to mutter anything.

But that was beside the point.

Scarlet was going to play my dream part.

She was ruining my Toxic Sunset.

She was making me look like a clone of one of her horrible Glossy Posse friends.

She was flirting with the boy I liked.

Who knew what else she was up to? What was she doing in my house while I wasn't there? Being nice to Rosemary? Offering to clear the table? If I ever returned, would my mother expect me to be helpful and neat?

It was an outrage.

There was no limit to the destruction Scarlet could cause. She had to be stopped immediately.

Finally, at the end of the day, I confronted her at my locker.

"Hi, Lavender," she said with a suspicious amount of happiness in her voice.

"I see what you're doing," I told her. "Oh, I've been watching you. I demand that you stop meddling in my life, starting now."

"Meddling? What are you talking about?"

"These clothes, for one thing." I made a face at the new sweater, the jeans, hair. "Oh my gosh — are you wearing lip gloss?"

"Do you like it?"

"No! I don't wear lip gloss! Why are you putting it on my lips? And *what have you done with my glasses?*"

"Lavender, please calm down," she said. "I'm only trying to help. You know, if you just make a teensy effort to take care of yourself and be nice to people, it makes a big difference."

"That sounds like something you'd say," I snapped.

"Well, I can't help it. I don't want to walk around with tangled hair and sloppy clothes. I'm stuck in your body for now, so I figure I might as well make the best of it." She took a step back so I could see her better. "Besides, don't you like these new clothes even a little? You'll get to keep them if we ever switch back. I think they look pretty good."

I swept my eyes over her and tried to think of something sarcastic to say. But I couldn't. I hated to admit it, but I did kind of like some of the changes she'd made. The barrettes were cute. The platforms made me taller. And the sweater was a pretty shade of blue.

"They're okay, I guess."

I didn't like the way she smiled when I said that. Like we were starting to become friends or something.

The trouble was, here I was in this extremely weird situation, and nobody, not even Maybelle, could possibly understand what I was going through. Nobody but Scarlet.

We needed each other.

"I'd better go," Scarlet said. "I've got a cast meeting with Mr. B., and I want to stop in the art room to pick up your painting before I go —"

Hmmm . . . why? Maybe she thought John would be there?

"It's my painting," I said. "I'll get it for you."

"Thanks, Lavender! See you at rehearsal." She skipped off to the auditorium. It was important for her to be on time for rehearsal, but I had such a tiny part nobody would notice if I was a few minutes late.

The art studio was empty except for John, who sat at an easel, drawing.

I crept up behind him. "What are you working on?"

"Hey — Scarlet." His cheek twitched. I'd startled him. "I'm sketching some ideas for *The Music Man*. I volunteered to help build the sets."

"Is this Marian's living room?" I asked. "Where she gives piano lessons?"

"Yeah. It's not finished yet."

The sketch showed a piano, some fusty Victorian furniture, and on the wall, a portrait of a Hawaiian man wearing a lei.

"Hey," I said. "Is that . . . Hawaiian music guru Don Ho?"

"You like Don Ho?" John asked.

"Yes," I said.

"Lavender likes Don Ho."

"I know."

"I thought, since she's playing Marian, she'd like to have a picture of Don Ho in her living room, so the set feels like home to her."

His gesture was so sweet it gave me a stomachache. A strange, good stomachache. The experience was so baffling it temporarily erased my ability to speak. I moved my mouth but no words came out.

"Mr. Brummel doesn't want the Don Ho picture in Marian's living room," John said. "He says it's wrong for the period of the play. That's true, but the audience will never notice."

I still couldn't speak.

"Hardly anybody knows who Don Ho is anymore," John said. "Except for Lavender. And me. And . . . you, I guess." He looked at me as if he wasn't quite sure who I was. His cheek twitched again. "We're an exclusive club. Don Ho is our secret password."

"I hope you keep the Don Ho picture on the set." My power of speech had returned. "Does Lavender know about it?"

"No," John said. "It's a surprise."

"She'll like it."

"I hope so."

Was it possible he — no, I wouldn't let myself even think it.

"Lavender's a great singer," I said. "Don't you think so?"

"Sure," John said. "And she's cute too."

The stomachache returned, just for a second. "You think Lavender is cute?"

"Well, sure," John said. "She's okay."

Oh, I thought. *Only okay?*

"Lavender *is* cute," I said. "Not just okay."

"You know, Scarlet, you're a lot nicer than you seem from a distance."

"I've made a big effort recently," I said. "To improve my character."

"That's very admirable."

He continued sketching. I watched. For a few moments the only sound in the room was his pencil scratching the paper.

"Are you going to the Spooktacular?" I asked.

"I don't know yet." John looked up from his work. "Are you?"

"I don't know either," I said. "I have a boy in mind, but there are complications."

"What kind of complications?"

"I can't get into it now."

"Very mysterious." John's cheek twitched a third time.

"Are you all right?" I asked him. "Your cheek keeps twitching."

"I'm okay," he said. "I'm feeling a little confused, that's all."

"It happens," I said. "I completely understand."

18

Chemistry

Mr. Brummel held the first rehearsal for *The Music Man* on Thursday afternoon, the day the cast list was posted. "We've got no time to waste," he explained. "We open December twelfth. That gives us only a month and a half to learn all our lines and songs and dance steps."

A murmur ran through the cast as we realized how much work we had ahead of us.

Mr. Brummel summed up the story: Professor Harold Hill is a traveling salesman who comes to River City, Iowa, selling marching band instruments and uniforms. He convinces the townspeople that the children need a marching band. But Harold Hill is a con man who doesn't know the first thing about music, and Marian Paroo, the librarian and piano teacher, is onto him. Before the instruments arrive he pretends to teach the kids to play using his patented "Think System": All they have to do is think of a tune over and over and it will come out of the instrument when they play it. He plans to skip town before everyone realizes that the kids don't know how to play music at all. But when the time comes he can't leave, because he and Marian have fallen in love. And even though the band is terrible, the kids' parents think it sounds wonderful, and Harold is a hero.

"So in a way," Mr. Brummel finished, "the Think System worked. The kids thought so hard about the music that they had the confidence to play it, and their parents wanted so badly to see their children in a marching band that they heard real music when it played. Thinking made it true."

Everyone was silent for a moment. *Thinking made it true.* I knew that wasn't possible, and yet . . . I had made a wish, and here I was in Lavender's body. I didn't know how or why, but . . . could simple *thinking* have made it happen?

"I want you to bring all your energy to your roles, no matter how big or small," Mr. Brummel said. "Now let's begin the read-through."

The lead cast members sat in a circle with Mr. Brummel while the chorus made an outer ring around us. The chorus didn't have much to do but listen while we read our lines. Lavender came in a little late, carrying her Toxic Sunset. She sat down in an empty seat right behind me. Charlie, who was sitting next to me, turned his head and smiled shyly at her. Then he caught sight of her painting.

"Scarlet — did you paint that?"

Lavender set the painting on her lap to show it to him proudly. "Well, yes, I —" Something in his face must have stopped her. I guess he didn't expect the Scarlet he knew to paint a toxic sunset. I'd tried to lighten it up but it was still pretty hideous.

"This is Lavender's painting," Lavender finished. "I'm holding it for her while she rehearses."

"Oh." Charlie looked relieved. Reality as he knew it was restored.

"I really love the combination of black and green," I said, doing my best Lavender imitation. "It's so ugly it's beautiful."

Charlie nodded warily, as if he were humoring a crazy person.

"I sure wish *I* had painted it," Lavender said. I kicked her under the chair. I never would have said that. She was not doing a very good job of being me.

Then we started reading the play. After my first few lines, Lavender leaned forward and whispered in my ear, "Make Marian prissier. She's very uptight at first."

I tightened up my tone and saw Mr. Brummel nod happily.

Lavender kept giving me little secret tips, which helped a lot. But after a while I didn't need them anymore. For a few blissful moments my confusion melted away. I wasn't Scarlet *or* Lavender — I was Marian. And Charlie was Harold Hill. And we were in love.

"Charlie, let's hear a little more feeling," Mr. Brummel said when we got near the end. Harold Hill was telling Marion he loved her, but now that Mr. Brummel mentioned it, Charlie did seem to be holding back. His head kept tilting to the left, toward Lavender, as if he couldn't quite forget that she was sitting there.

He thinks she's me, I kept reminding myself. *That's a good thing.*

"You two have real chemistry," Mr. Brummel said to us. "Who could have predicted it? I must be a casting genius."

Charlie and I had chemistry — even when I was Lavender! I looked at the floor and pinched my lips together, trying not to smile.

"Lavender — you were wonderful," Mr. Brummel added.

Ow! Behind me, the real Lavender secretly pinched the back of my neck. What was she so mad about? She was lucky she'd made the chorus, with *her* voice.

"You were too, Charlie," Mr. Brummel said. "I'm sure you'll relax into the role once you get to know Lavender better."

"Nice work, *Lavender*," Lavender said when rehearsal broke up. "Here's your painting." She plopped the Toxic Sunset into my arms.

"Thank you so much, *Scarlet*," I said. "But you know what? Why don't you keep it? It's my gift to you."

"Excellent." Lavender grinned and took the painting back. "I'll hang it up in my room."

"Give it to your stepbrother, Ben," I said in a fakey-sweet voice. "He likes that kind of thing."

"Actually, you're right," Lavender said. "Ben could probably use a present from you — I mean, me."

"That's not what I meant," I said. "He's mean to you. He doesn't deserve anything nice from you."

She looked at me for a long second. "You're wrong about him."

"What's that supposed to mean?"

"Lavender!" Mr. Brummel called. "I need to see you for a minute."

"Call me later." Lavender walked off with the painting, while I went to see Mr. Brummel.

Mr. Brummel pulled me and Charlie aside. "We'll have to set up some extra rehearsals, just the three of us. After all, you have a big responsibility. The entire musical rests on your shoulders."

I shuddered. I was thrilled to be a star, but to think that everyone was depending on me . . . well, that scared me a little.

Charlie and I walked out of the auditorium together. "Looks like we're going to be pretty busy," he said.

"I don't mind," I said. "I like rehearsing."

He nodded, hiding behind his hair. "So . . . what are you going to be for Halloween?"

"I don't know yet," I said. I hadn't really thought about Halloween, even though it was only two days away.

"Are you going to the Spooktacular?"

"Probably. But I don't have a date yet." *Hint hint.* "Are you going?"

"I hope so."

I waited for him to say more. We stood awkwardly in the lobby, electricity crackling between us.

What if he asks me to the dance? I thought. *Now, while I'm Lavender? Would that be good or bad?*

Good, if I was still Lavender on Saturday.

Bad, if we found a way to switch back by then.

Switching back was looking less and less likely. So far Lavender and I had no idea how to do it.

"Lavender, there's something I want to ask you," Charlie said.

Oh my gosh! I thought. *This is it!*

My imagination went into overdrive. First I'd go to the Spooktacular with Charlie. Then we'd star in the musical together. After that, who knows?

"About the Spooktacular —"

"Yes?" I swallowed hard to keep my heart from springing out of my mouth.

"I really like you, Lavender," Charlie said. "And I was wondering . . . would you put in a good word for me? With Scarlet?"

My heart stopped. What? What was he talking about?

"I've had a mad crush on her since last year," Charlie confessed. "She's so cute! But she always seemed kind of hard to talk to. Out of my league. I've wanted to ask her out for a while, but I was afraid to."

My head started spinning. This was so confusing!

Charlie had a crush on Scarlet. On me. The girl who was Scarlet last year — that was me. . . .

"But Scarlet's been different lately," Charlie said.

"Not that she wasn't nice before, but you know . . . she's easier to talk to now. . . ."

I tried to catch my breath. Charlie had liked me all this time, and I never knew it?

"I think I might try to work up the courage to ask her to the dance," he said. "You know her pretty well, right? Do you think she'll say yes?"

What was I going to say? What was I going to do?

"Um, I don't know. . . ."

He was crazy about Scarlet. He just didn't know she was me!

"It would really help if you could clear the way for me, Lavender," he said. "Tell her I'm a good guy. See how she feels about me. So when I ask her I won't be so nervous I can't talk."

I made him so nervous he couldn't talk?!

This meant one thing, and one thing only: I had to get my old body back right away. By any means necessary.

"What do you say, Lavender? Will you help me?"

I will be Scarlet again, I promised myself. *By Saturday night, everything will be back to normal.*

It had to be.

"I'll do what I can," I said. "I can't make any promises. But I think you and Scarlet would make a great couple."

"Really? You do?"

I nodded. "She'll say yes. You don't need to be nervous around her."

He beamed. "Thanks, Lavender. You're the best." He practically skipped out of the auditorium.

As soon as he was gone, I jumped up and tried to kick my heels together. But of course I was Lavender so I ended up kicking myself in the butt and landing on my knee.

Still, I was happy. Thrilled. Charlie liked me! He wanted to take me to the Halloween Dance!

Me. Not Lavender.

I had to become myself again in time for the dance. If Lavender got to go with Charlie in my place, I'd have to kill her.

Switching meant I wouldn't get to star in the play. I'd be stuck in the chorus, dancing. No more lovely singing voice. No more rehearsals with Charlie. That part was sad.

But Lavender said she deserved the part, and maybe she did. It was her voice that had won it, after all.

I wouldn't get to kiss Charlie onstage. But maybe I'd get to kiss him in real life. And that was better.

Way better.

I crossed my fingers and prayed that I would be myself again by Halloween night.

If only I knew how.

19

Lonely

"Scarlet, aren't you coming to dinner?" Her mom tapped tentatively on the door as if she were afraid to stir the beast.

Now was when I missed my family the most. Dinnertime was miserable at Scarlet's house. I thought I was sick of Mom asking me about my day, and Rosemary telling funny stories about her classmates, and Dad pretending to be grouchy and making goofy jokes. I thought I was tired of planning how to decorate the house for every holiday (Dad was begging me and Rosemary to make Crab Cupids to put in the yard for Valentine's Day next year). My family wasn't as rich as Scarlet's and our house wasn't as nice, but at least my parents were always on my side. I didn't have to worry about being picked on while I ate.

"Scarlet," her mother said. "Answer me."

"Do I really have a choice?"

"Scarlet, none of your attitude or you're going to eat alone in your room."

"Fine. Send the chow on up."

"Scarlet! When did you get so coarse?"

"About three days ago." I had been stuck in Scarlet's body for three whole days, and it felt like forever.

I sat in my luxury prison, picking at the nubs on my bed-spread, replaying Day Three over and over in my head like a bad late-night movie.

The low point: rehearsal. Watching Scarlet read Marian's lines, the lines I'd dreamed of saying onstage since I was six, hurt even more than I'd expected. At first it was a weird thrill to see *me* — that is, my body, my Lavender body — playing Marian. But I was only watching. I didn't get to experience it myself.

I knew this situation was not Scarlet's fault. But there was a bigger problem, bigger than not getting to play Marian. The longer I lived apart from my own body, the more disconnected I felt from everyone and everything I knew. I was lonely.

I missed my old room. I missed Maybelle and John. I missed Mom's sloppy hugs and Dad's embarrassing teasing. I even missed Rosemary and her sniffly nose and sniffly comments.

Meanwhile, I was stuck with Scarlet's life. I'd left the Toxic Sunset on Scarlet's white dresser, leaning against the wall. It didn't look very good in her room. That fact gave me a kind of grim satisfaction. If we ever switched back, she could keep the painting as a reminder.

It was an angry painting, and it reminded me a little of the angry landscapes in Ben's video games. *Maybe he really would like it*, I thought.

So after dinner, which turned out to be something called *broiled Arctic char with wilted arugula*, I took the painting to Ben's room. I could hear the bangs and crashes of a game through the closed door. I knocked.

"What?" Ben shouted.

"It's Scarlet."

"What do you want?"

"Can you open the door?"

The war noises stopped as he paused the game and opened the door. "Is it your math homework? I told you, I don't remember any of that stuff."

"It's not math. It's this." I showed him the painting.

"What about it?"

"Do you like it? It's for you."

"What are you talking about?"

I stepped into his room, which was almost as neat as Scarlet's, only blue instead of white. "I painted this for you. Or actually, my friend Lavender painted it and I worked on it some too. I thought it would look good in your room."

He took the painting and held it up against a blank blue wall. "*You* painted this? It doesn't look like something you'd even *touch*."

I laughed. "Yeah, I know. But I'm trying to explore the dark corners of my mind."

He looked at me with new respect. "So what does it mean?"

"What does what mean?"

"The painting."

"Oh." What did it mean? When I'd started painting it I thought it meant something about how industry was hurting the environment. But there was more to it than that.

"It means I'm not feeling so happy," I said.

"What's wrong?"

"I miss my old life," I said. "But I don't know how to get it back."

He had no idea what I was talking about. There was no way he could really understand. But he surprised me.

"I know how you feel," he said. "I miss my old life too, before Dad and Leigh got married. It's not that Leigh's so bad. But I miss my mom."

"You don't have to defend Leigh to me," I said. "She's so worried about trying to please your dad she doesn't have much energy left to be a mother."

"Yeah, but at least she cares about you." Ben sat down hard on his bed, the springs bouncing under his weight. "My dad doesn't care about anybody but himself. I'm pretty sure that's why my mom left."

"He's a bully," I said.

He looked up at me. "Yeah. You're right."

"I think he wants us to fight," I said. "He can control us that way. But what if we tried to get along better? We could be nicer to each other, and help each other out. That might make living in this family a little easier."

I thought about my mother and Rosemary, and the careless way I'd treated them. I'd never done much to make my own family happier. It was easier to see the problems when they belonged to somebody else's family.

"You know, when Dad and Leigh got married, I thought the worst part about it was going to be putting up with you, Princess," Ben said. "But I'm starting to think you're not so bad."

Not exactly high praise, but it was a start.

"Thanks for the painting," he added. He pulled a toolbox out of his closet and got busy hanging it up on his wall.

Scarlet called me late that night.

"Charlie's going to ask Scarlet to the Spooktacular," she told me. "Which, right now, means you."

"Oh, no," I said. "I don't want to go with him. I want to go with John."

"Did John ask you?"

"No."

"I told Charlie you'd say yes," Scarlet said.

"Why did you do that?"

"Because I really want to go with him."

"But — he's going to ask *me*."

"He's not asking *you*. He's asking *Scarlet*."

"But he thinks I'm Scarlet!"

"I know."

"This makes me very queasy," I said.

"Listen," Scarlet said. "I've thought about this a lot. And there's nothing else to do. When Charlie asks you to the dance, say yes. Then we'll cross our fingers and hope that by Saturday night, we've switched bodies again."

"But we have no reason to think that will happen," I said.

"We've just got to have faith. We've got to believe that somehow it will all work out."

"Do you believe that?" I asked.

"Not really," Scarlet admitted.

"The Think System," I said.

"What?"

"Like in the musical," I explained. "Harold Hill's patented Think System. We'll have to try it. Right now it's all we've got."

"That's not much."

"I know it isn't."

"I'd better go," she said. "Your mom's knocking on the door."

"Kiss her good night for me," I said. "And Dad too."

"I will," Scarlet said. "Kiss my mom for me."

"Okay," I said. "Oh, and, um — I gave the Toxic Sunset to Ben."

"You did? Why would you do that?"

"I thought he would like it."

"What did he do, spit on it? Kick a hole through it?"

"No. He thanked me."

She was silent for a second. "That's it? He just said 'thank you'?"

"And then we had a little talk. I think he's lonely, Scarlet."

"Of course he is," Scarlet scoffed. "He's mean; he's gross; he's not nearly as funny as he thinks he is. Why would anybody like him?"

"He's not so bad if you take the time to talk to him."

"That sound you don't hear is my eyes rolling."

"Maybe you never noticed, but Steve is even meaner to Ben than he is to you."

"And I'm supposed to care . . . why?"

"Because if you think about it, you and Ben are on the same team. You can help each other, defend each other —"

"Yeah, and then he'll turn on me."

"I don't think he will," I said. "I think he needs you."

She was quiet again.

"And maybe you need him," I added.

"Mom's not very helpful."

"No, she isn't."

"I'll think about it," Scarlet said. "In the meantime, you're there and I'm here, and we don't know how to change it."

"That's true. But whatever happens, we have each other."

"We have each other."

Small comfort. But a comfort nevertheless.

20

A Fortune-Teller

Lavender's words still rang in my head when I woke up the next morning. Was it really true that Ben needed me?

I tried to imagine life at home without Ben and me sniping at each other. It wouldn't be perfect, but it would be a lot better.

I also thought about Lavender's feelings about the way I'd been dressing lately. Maybe I had gone a little too far too quickly. I wore sneakers instead of the platforms — I was always tripping in those anyway. But I still fixed her hair nicely and wore the new jeans. Lavender was just going to have to get used to looking good. And I'd teach her how to put in contact lenses.

She was waiting for me at her locker. I'd texted her some French phrases the night before to help her get through class, spelled phonetically so she'd know how to pronounce them. And she'd sent me some Spanish phrases in return.

"*Bonjour*, Lavender, *comment allez-vous?*"

She blinked at me. Still sleepy, I guess. Then she said, "Oh! I get it. *Très bien*, thanks. *¿Cómo éstas?*"

"*Très bien, merci.* Don't forget the *merci.*"

"*Merci, merci.* Now your turn: *Buenos días,* Scarlet. *¿Cómo estás?*"

A little more language practice and we were ready for the day. "Let me know if anything happens with Charlie," I told her.

"I will. And don't flirt too much with John!"

"But I'm being *you* when I flirt with John."

"It still bugs me," Lavender said.

"Schmitzy!" Maybelle rushed up to me before art class later that day, her face flushed and smiling. "He asked me!"

"Who?" I asked. "Ian?"

Maybelle nodded. "He was afraid to ask unless he knew for sure I didn't have another date."

"So the note really was from him?"

"Yep."

Whew. I was relieved that Zoe wasn't behind it. But what would happen when word got out that Ian had asked Maybelle to the Spooktacular and not Zoe? I shuddered to think. An unhappy Zoe was a mean Zoe.

"Have you told anyone else?" I asked.

"Who else would I tell?" Maybelle said. "You're my best friend."

"Maybe you should keep the news quiet for the rest of

the day," I suggested. The longer it took for Zoe to find out, the less time she'd have for planning revenge.

"Okay," Maybelle said. "But why? Oh." She frowned. "Schmitzy, you don't have a date yet, do you? You can come with me and Ian. We'll all go together. John will be there too. You can dance with him."

Everyone had a date except for me. "You and Ian go alone. I'm sure he doesn't want me hanging around."

"He will if he wants *me* hanging around," Maybelle said. "The Spooktacular wouldn't be fun without you." Her face suddenly brightened at something behind my back.

Someone tapped me on the shoulder. I turned and there stood John Obrycki.

"I've got to run," Maybelle said, giggling. "See you later." She disappeared into the art room.

"Hi, John," I said.

"Hi, Lavender." John's cheek twitched. "I made this for you." He opened his hand to show me a folded-paper fortune-teller.

Most people made fortune-tellers with four colors on the outside, eight numbers on the inside, and a different fortune under each number. You picked a color — say, red. The person telling your fortune moved the paper contraption with his fingers, opening and closing the paper three times — R-E-D. Then you picked a number — say, two — and the fortune-teller moved the paper again, twice, counting it out, one-two. You looked inside and lifted a flap. Your fortune was written underneath.

John's fortune-teller was different. Instead of colors on the four outside squares, he'd drawn flowers. The purple one was a lavender flower. I recognized it from the wrapper on the lavender soap my mother used.

"That's the prettiest fortune-teller I ever saw," I said.

He slipped the fortune-teller over his fingers and thumbs. "Look inside. It tells a special fortune just for you."

Each flap had a number, one through eight.

"Lift the flaps in order," John said. "Starting with Number One." I reached inside and lifted the flap marked *1.* Underneath it said, *Will.*

"Keep going," John prompted.

I picked up flap number 2. It said, *You.*

Then *Go,*

    To,

        The,

            Dance,

                With,

                    Me?

I didn't know what to say. This was one of the sweetest things I'd ever seen. But it wasn't meant for me, not really. It was meant for Lavender.

"So — will you?" He studied my face for an answer. I could see the nervousness and worry in his eyes, and that made the whole thing even sweeter. "Did it read in the right order? Maybe I folded the paper wrong —"

"You folded it perfectly," I told him.

"*And?*"

I had to answer for Lavender. She'd said on the phone that she wanted to go with John. And she'd be a fool to say no.

"The answer is yes. I'd love to go to the dance with you."

"Great!" He flashed a goofy grin. "Well, see you later." He ran down the hall, jumping up to tap the Exit sign with his hand on the way.

My dream was to go to the Spooktacular with Charlie. But if I couldn't have that — if I was still stuck in Lavender's body by then — a girl could do a lot worse than John.

21

Zoe's Plan

"I've got a little present to pass along to you," Scarlet said. "Hold out your hand."

I held out my hand. She dropped a beautifully decorated origami fortune-teller into my palm. I knew right away it was from John. Origami, for one thing. And the daisy. He always drew his daisies in red, like hearts. But it was the purple sprig of lavender that really got me.

I read the question buried under the flaps and flushed red. "He asked you?"

"He asked *you*," Scarlet replied.

"Did his cheek twitch?" I asked. "When he asked you?"

"What do you mean?"

"I mean like this." I demonstrated a John cheek twitch. I'd been practicing it in the mirror, just for kicks.

"Yeah, a little," Scarlet said. "What's up with that?"

"A nervous tic. Isn't it cute?"

"What about Charlie?" Scarlet asked. "Did he ask you yet?"

"This morning," I replied. "In the library."

She nearly jumped out of her skin. "What did he say? Tell me every detail."

I set the scene for her. Charlie had approached me in the library, hiding behind his hair and obviously nervous. He wouldn't let me see his eyes, but his hands were trembling just the tiniest bit. He said, "Scarlet, can I ask you something?" It still took me a second to get used to being called Scarlet. I was about to say, "Sure," when he cleared his throat really loudly and said, "Um, Scarlet?" His voice cracked just at that moment, and the librarian shushed him.

"How dare she?" the real Scarlet said to me now. "How dare she shush a boy at such a crucial moment!"

"Ms. Aguilar didn't know it was a crucial moment. Anyway, after that he whispered, because she was giving us the stinkeye."

"And? What did he whisper?" Scarlet was really worked up about this date thing.

"He said, 'Would you like to go to the Spooktacular? With me, I mean?'"

"Those were his exact words?"

"Exact words."

She leaned back and dreamily mouthed the words to herself — committing them to memory, I suppose. Then she snapped back to reality. "So you said yes, of course. Please tell me you said yes, Lavender."

"Actually, I said, 'I'll go with you if you shave your head and dye it blue.'"

"You did not." The blood drained out of her face.

"No, I didn't." I couldn't keep teasing her when I saw how much this meant to her. "I said yes, that would be nice, blabbity blah."

"I wish I could have been there," Scarlet said.

"I know how you feel," I said. "I wish I could have seen John's cheek twitch."

"So here we are," Scarlet said. "We both have dates to the dance. Just not the right ones."

"Yeah." I fiddled with the fortune-teller John had made. I wished it really *could* tell the future.

"Scarlet! You'll never guess what I heard," Zoe said during study hall. The study hall teacher had left us on our honor to be quiet, the fool.

"What?" I asked.

"Lavender Schmitz is going to the Halloween Spooktacular," Zoe said.

"With a *date*," Kelsey chimed in.

"Gee, that's shocking," I said.

"I *know*," Zoe said, my sarcasm whizzing over her head. "Of course, her date is a loser. But even John Obrycki can do better than *Lavender*."

"Do you have a date yet, Zoe?" I asked.

She bristled. "Not officially. But Ian Colburn is going to ask me any minute. It's all over the school."

"He's just trying to work up the courage," Kelsey said.

"Keep telling yourself that," I mumbled.

"What about you, Scarlet?" Zoe asked. "Who are you going with?"

"As if you don't know," I said. Someone had seen Charlie whispering to me in the library and soon everybody was talking about it. The gossip in our school was unbelievable.

"You can't trust everything you hear," Zoe said. "I'd like to get the news directly from you."

"You used to tell us everything," Kelsey said.

"You're anti-Charlie," I told them. "That's why I didn't tell you."

"I'm not anti-Charlie," Zoe said. "I just think you should leave him to the theater geeks and go with someone like Ian. Not Ian himself, of course — I've got dibs — but someone *like* him."

"Zoe, you forget — Scarlet's one of the theater geeks herself now," Kelsey said.

"Oh, that's right," Zoe said. "How is it in the *chorus*?"

"Superb," I said.

Whenever I said something un-Scarlet-ish, Zoe paused to study me as if she wasn't sure she knew me anymore. And, of course, she didn't. I could see her trying to shake off the weird feeling she was getting from me.

"You know what? I don't care who you go to the dance with," she finally said. "Charlie's adorable. I admit it. Let's call a truce. The three of us and our dates will all go to the dance together. Okay?"

I leaned back and crossed my long legs. For the first time in my life, crossing my legs felt natural. "Why on earth would I want to do that?"

There was that look again. My snappy comebacks were stunning Zoe silent. Temporarily.

Not Kelsey, though. Nothing could quiet her. "Because," Kelsey explained, "Zoe has an excellent idea. Something that will make the dance extra fun."

I uncrossed my legs and leaned forward. "I can't wait to hear all about it."

"People like Lavender going to the dance — with *dates*," Zoe said. "It's not right. It will ruin the dance."

"Why?" I asked.

"It just will," Kelsey said.

"Don't you think dances are more fun when everyone has dates?" I asked.

"No," Zoe replied. "If everyone has dates, who will take tickets at the door? Who will work behind the snack table?"

"We need people like Lavender and the other canines to stay in their place so the rest of us can have fun," Kelsey explained.

"Stay in their place?" I said. "But the Spooktacular is for everyone."

"That's the official party line," Zoe said. "Teachers have to say that, legally. No one believes it."

"You know, Zoe, you're starting to talk like a James Bond villain," I said. " 'Soon, Mr. Bond, ve vill destroy everyvon in ze school, and ze dance vill be for me and me alone!' "

"You've become a total freak, Scarlet," Kelsey said.

"Will you please stop being weird and listen to the plan?" Zoe said.

I propped my chin on my hand and awaited the gory details.

"We'll humiliate Lavender at the dance," Zoe said. "Maybe some kind of stink spray? Something that will make all the boys think twice before they ask her to a dance again."

"That's your plan?" It seemed to me they hadn't given this plan much thought. So I wasn't that worried.

"We're still working out the kinks," Kelsey said.

"The best part is, it's a costume party," Zoe said. "So we can't get into trouble. If our costumes are good enough, no one will know who we are."

"I'm not worried about getting into trouble," I said. "I just don't think it's a good idea."

"Can you think of a better one?" Kelsey asked.

"How about this: Let's leave Lavender alone. And try to have a good time without hurting anyone?"

Kelsey wrinkled her nose. "That's boring."

"You've changed, Scarlet," Zoe said. "You used to be fun. What are you, running for Pope?"

"I'd consider it," I said. "But they usually pick an old man." I probably should have held back on the wisecracks, because Zoe gave me another one of those suspicious looks. "Anyway, you can do what you want. I'm not going to help you."

"Yes, you are," Zoe said.

"No, I'm not," I said.

"Yes, you are, Scarlet," Zoe repeated.

"Why should I?"

"Because if you don't," Zoe said, "we'll tell everyone about You-Know-What."

You-Know-What?

"What are you talking about?" I asked.

Kelsey gave a short laugh. "Don't pretend you don't know."

I didn't, of course. But I figured Scarlet did.

How bad could it be? I wasn't going to be blackmailed by Zoe. "I don't care," I said. "Go ahead and tell everybody about whatever it is."

"You don't care?" Zoe said. "You should. If Charlie hears what you did, he won't like you anymore. And your new friends Lavender, Maybelle, and John will never forgive you."

"If you want to have any friends left by Thanksgiving," Kelsey said, "you'll help us."

Hmmm, I thought. *What in the world could Scarlet have done that was this bad?* She was thoughtless sometimes, but so far she didn't strike me as out-and-out evil. Maybe I didn't know her as well as I thought I did. But if you couldn't get to know someone through and through by living in her body, living in her house, sleeping in her bed, living her entire life for her . . . if that wasn't enough to know someone else's secrets, how could anyone ever hope to?

"We're just going to play a little joke on Lavender," Zoe said. "She won't mind. She enjoys the attention."

"How do you know?" I asked. There were many things I did not enjoy. One of them was attention. Especially mean attention.

"She told me once," Zoe said.

Liar.

Maybe Zoe was bluffing. I hoped so. But I needed to find out what this You-Know-What thing was — fast.

"So, you'll help us prank Lavender, right, Scarlet?" Kelsey said.

"I'll get back to you," I told them.

Zoe scowled. "Let us know by tomorrow night, or we'll tell everyone about You-Know-What the next day."

"And then you might as well transfer to another school," Kelsey said. "Because you won't have a friend at Falls Road."

I had to find Scarlet right away.

22

You-Know-What

Lavender stopped me on my way into the auditorium. "Scarlet? I need to talk to you."

A little hope rose in my heart. Maybe she'd figured out a way to switch us back to our old selves! But there was a grim look in her eyes that made me nervous.

"Let's go inside." I tugged on the auditorium door. "We're late for rehearsal."

"This won't take long." Lavender gave me a searing stare. I let the door go. "I have a little question for you."

Inside I squirmed, but I tried not to let it show. "Ask away."

"Okay." Now Lavender shifted from one leg to the other. She looked uncomfortable. This whole conversation was giving me a dreadful feeling. "Here's what I want to ask you: What's You-Know-What?"

"What?"

"What's You-Know-What?"

"I don't know," I said . . . but that heavy, dreadful feeling spread through my stomach. Did I know? Maybe I did. "What are you talking about?"

"Well, Zoe wants me to play a little joke at the dance," Lavender said.

"What kind of joke?" I knew Zoe's "jokes." This was bad. I grabbed her arm — *my* arm. It felt surprisingly bony. She shook off my hand.

"A joke on you. On 'Lavender.' Zoe says if I don't help her, she'll tell everyone about You-Know-What." Lavender swallowed hard. "What is she talking about, Scarlet? I think I should know."

The dreadful feeling hardened into a boulder and dropped with a thud in the pit of my stomach.

I knew exactly what You-Know-What was. I'd tried to forget about it, but now I realized that deep down I'd been afraid it would come back to haunt me someday. And now that day was here.

The auditorium door popped open and Mr. Brummel poked his head out. "Lavender, let's go. Time for rehearsal. You too, Scarlet."

"We'll be right there," I said. Mr. Brummel's head disappeared and the door swung shut.

"Well?" Lavender crossed her arms and glared at me. "Are you going to tell me?"

I didn't want to tell her. I wished I could pretend I knew nothing about it. But she was bound to find out sooner or later.

After four days in her body I couldn't help feeling connected to her. We were sisters, in a way. And now . . .

"You're going to hate me," I said. I took a deep breath

and braced myself for the fallout. "Okay." I paused. "Okay." I paused again. "Okay —"

"Scarlet! Spit it out!"

"Okay. Remember that rumor that went around a while ago, back in September?"

"About me?" Lavender asked. "Which one? The one that said my real father is a gorilla and I have to visit him at the zoo every other weekend according to a custody agreement?"

"No." I had nothing to do with that.

"The one that said Pepe's Pizza hired me to play Barney at birthday parties because I don't need a dinosaur suit?"

"No." I swallowed. "The one that said your hair's so thick you can't go to a normal salon because their equipment can't handle the job." I hesitated, hating to go on. "So you have to go to a dog groomer instead." I swallowed again. My mouth was dry.

"Yes?" Lavender wouldn't let me off the hook.

"So somebody put a bumper sticker on your locker that said I GOT SHAVED AT DOTTIE'S DOG-TOPIA. And the sticker wouldn't come off?"

"And I got detention for having a sticker on my locker?" Lavender said. (We weren't allowed to put stickers on our lockers.) "And they had to call the janitor to get it off, and he made a big show of scrubbing my locker while everybody laughed?" She frowned. "Yes, I remember that."

"Well," I croaked. "That was me."

Lavender said nothing.

"I made up the joke. About the dog groomer. Zoe and I were goofing around and the joke just popped out of my mouth."

Lavender held very still, as if trying to keep her face from crumpling. I wished she would say something.

"I stood watch while Zoe put the bumper sticker on your locker, but that wasn't my idea." I said. "And I didn't spread the joke all over school. Zoe did that."

"All you did was make up the joke," Lavender said. "About me going to a dog groomer."

It sounded bad when she put it that way. I wished I could take those words back.

"I didn't mean anything by it, Lavender," I swore. "The joke was stupid. I didn't think about how much it would hurt you."

Mr. Brummel appeared again. "Ladies, while we're young . . . ?"

"Go in," Lavender said. "They need you. You're the star."

"What about you?" I said. "They need you too."

"Not today. Mr. B. won't miss me."

I wanted to go into rehearsal, but my feet felt glued to the floor.

"Lavender," I said. "I'm really sorry. Seriously sorry. Completely, utterly, and totally sorry."

Her face — my face — looked so solemn, so deeply sad. It was an expression I'd never seen on my own face before. An expression I didn't think my face could make, until now.

"I thought we were friends," she said.

"We *are* friends!" I insisted.

"No, we're not. Not anymore."

Lavender turned her back on me and left. I watched her walk down the hall and out the door. I couldn't move.

A cloud descended upon me, heavy and suffocating. I'd hurt *her*, but I felt the pain.

I stood outside the auditorium, paralyzed, until Mr. Brummel took me by the arm and pulled me inside.

23

Smarties vs. Dum Dums

It was my own fault, really. I let my guard down. I should have known better.

I never should have trusted one of *them*.

How could I ever have thought Scarlet and I were friends? Or friendly, even?

Anyone who'd do something so mean — anyone who was best friends with Zoe and Kelsey — was deep down bad.

After my confrontation with Scarlet, I went home. To her home. Which didn't make me feel any better.

I found a box of brownie mix in a cupboard — I was amazed to find anything edible in there, other than a jar of capers, whatever they were — and made myself a big pan of brownies. When Ben came home I offered him one, even though I could easily have eaten them all myself.

"I didn't know you knew how to make brownies," Ben said.

"Ben, you are about to get an education."

"What's that supposed to mean?"

"It means that Scarlet's dark side is coming out."

"Should I be scared?" He was laughing lightly, joking, but the look on my face made him stop.

I was starting to scare him.

Good, I thought. *He should be scared.*

Everyone should be.

Except for John and Maybelle. The two people who have never betrayed me. So far.

Everyone else: Watch out.

In the meantime, I had a dance to get ready for. Scarlet's mother wanted to take me shopping for a dress, but the Spooktacular was a costume party, so I dragged her to a costume shop instead.

"Maybe you could go as a princess," she said. "Or a bride. Or a fairy! Maybe an angel . . . Then we could still pick out a nice gown for you. Something sparkly!"

"I'm going as a hula dancer," I said. I'd always wanted to wear a hula skirt — it went so well with my ukulele — but was afraid people would laugh at me. Especially since my belly was as white and squishy as a loaf of Wonder Bread.

But now I had Scarlet's lean brown belly, still tan from the summer. The perfect hula belly.

Scarlet's mother made a face. "A hula dancer? Well, I suppose it's cute."

I rented a grass skirt and a coconut top and a wreath of flowers for my hair and lots of leis.

"How about a ukulele?" the man in the costume shop said. "No self-respecting hula girl goes without one."

I looked at the cheap plywood uke he offered me. It wasn't nearly as nice as the vintage 1950s beauty I had at home.

"No thanks," I said. "I've already got one."

I'd bring my own uke to the party if I had to break into my bedroom and steal it.

Friday night. I was in Scarlet's room when I heard a noise at my bedroom window. I sat still and listened. There it was again. *Ping.*

I listened some more. A pebble hit my bedroom window. Then another. I went to the window. Scarlet was standing at the side of the house, tossing pebbles. I opened the window.

"Scarlet!" Scarlet called. "I need to talk to you. Please?"

"No," I shouted. "Go away."

"Please!" Scarlet cried. "I'm sorry!"

"Leave me alone." I shut the window and sat grumpily on the bed.

"Scarlet! Scarlet!" Scarlet shouted." I was wrong! I admit it! I've learned my lesson! Please talk to me!"

I shut the blind and covered my head with a pillow so I couldn't hear her.

Then my cell phone rang, a hip-hop ringtone. If I could have figured out how to change it to "The Hukilau Song," I would have.

"Hello?"

"Lavender, it's me. Listen — Zoe is playing us. Both of us. We have to stick together —"

Click. I hung up on her. She called back again and again. But I didn't answer. And I didn't listen to her messages.

I was not about to let Zoe play me. Or Scarlet either.

I was used to being alone. Besides, I needed all the time I could get to try to find a cure for my biggest problem: Scarlet-itis.

I was sick of being Scarlet Martinez. Sick of living with her uptight family.

There had to be a way to change back. But I was beginning to lose hope. Maybe I'd be Scarlet for the rest of my life.

That meant no more music. No more singing. I'd have to learn to like sports.

Maybe I could convince Scarlet's mom to send me to boarding school. Boarding school was expensive, but I felt pretty sure Steve would be happy to pay for it if it got me out of his house.

Being Scarlet wasn't all bad. There was Charlie. He was a good guy. I liked him. I could get used to kissing him, I supposed.

It wasn't his fault he wasn't John.

The next day was Halloween. Scarlet's mother put a plastic pumpkin by the front door and filled a crystal bowl with mini chocolate bars and bags of M&M's. I'll say this for her — she gave out excellent treats. My mother usually bought second-tier stuff like Smarties and Dum Dums. She liked the contrasting names — her idea of a joke. That wasn't as bad as Dad's idea of a joke, which was putting an inflatable "outhouse" on the front lawn. The door popped open to reveal a skeleton — with a crab for a head, of course — on the toilet, while speakers he rigged up played "Monster Mash" all night long.

Our house was a very popular stop on Halloween night.

Ben had plans to go out with his friend Vartek and "cause trouble," whatever that meant. He dressed up as a zombie.

"Brraaaiiinnns!" he growled when he zombied into the kitchen to show us his costume — basically beat-up, torn clothes rubbed with dirt to look as if they'd been decaying in a grave. He'd painted his face pale green with fake scars, lots of black around his eyes, and gummi worms coming out of his ears and hair. I laughed and dodged his flailing arms.

"Aren't you getting a little old for Halloween, Ben?" Steve said.

Ben froze, then dropped his arms to his sides and gave up the zombie act.

"You're right, Ben," I said. "No brains to be found in here. Better look somewhere else. Have you tried NASA?"

He grinned and placed one greenish hand on my head. "I'd eat yours, except I know they're made of plastic."

This would have bothered me a couple of days earlier, but now — the teasing way he said it, and the friendly way he clonked me on the head — it was more like an in-joke than a dis. Brother-sister stuff.

Steve got up to go, pulling on his driving gloves. "I've got a golf game. Leigh's upstairs resting — another one of her headaches. Try to do something productive today, Ben — don't waste the whole afternoon on video games. And Scarlet, don't spend the whole day on the phone, or whatever it is you do."

Ben and I munched Halloween candy while we watched Steve walk out of the house, get into his car, and zoom out of the driveway. Once he was safely gone, Ben said, "If you need me, I'll be in my room wasting the afternoon on video games. I guess you'll be on the phone?"

"Guess so. If Steve said so, it must be true."

We shared a bitter laugh and disappeared into our private domains.

Charlie called to make last-minute plans for the dance. "I'll pick you up at seven," he said. "What's your costume? Or is it a secret?"

"It's not a secret," I said. "I'm going as a hula girl."

"I'll be a surfer. Then our outfits will go together."

"Okay," I said.

"Lavender's upset, you know," he told me. "She was a mess during rehearsal yesterday. All flustered. Whenever I mentioned your name, she kind of flinched. Did you two have a fight?"

"She did something horrible to me," I said.

"*Lavender* did?" Charlie said. "She can be a little sarcastic, but I can't imagine her doing anything horrible to anyone."

"Well, she did. Unforgivable. And I consider myself to be a very forgiving person."

"She told me to tell you she wishes you could be friends again."

"I don't care."

"Scarlet, think about it," Charlie said. "Lavender's great. But she doesn't make friends as easily as you do."

Ha.

He went on. "Maybe you should cut her some slack — that's all I'm saying. Don't be a snob, Scarlet."

My spine went rigid. "Me, a snob! I'm not a snob! *She's* the snob!"

Charlie laughed. "Come on, Scarlet. Lavender a snob? Be real."

Be real? How could anyone call me *a snob?*

Charlie's words rattled me. I was Scarlet now. I had her looks, her friends, her grace, her social power. What had I done with them?

Not much. Certainly nothing good.

"Scarlet" snubbing "Lavender." That put us right back where we started.

I hung up the phone and sank down on Scarlet's bed. Charlie had given me a sudden realization, and it hurt.

Inside, I was no better than Scarlet.

24

A Mad Zoe Is a Mean Zoe

It was Halloween. The night of the Spooktacular. And Lavender still refused to speak to me.

She'd said Zoe was up to something. But what? I wondered if Lavender knew. And if she did, would she join in Zoe's scheme? Here was her chance to take revenge on me. Would she take it?

Or would she try to protect me, out of loyalty to her old self?

It was hard to say.

I wanted to be *my* old self again. I wanted to go to the dance with Charlie.

But if Zoe told everyone at the dance what I did to Lavender, Charlie would hate me. So would Maybelle and John.

Lavender already did.

I wished I could erase that stupid dog joke from everyone's memory. I never wanted to do or say anything mean again. To anyone.

But I couldn't erase it. And now it was coming back to haunt me.

All I could do was brace myself for the worst.

I dressed up as an alien. I covered my face in green makeup and wore a green wig with aluminum foil antennae. Rosemary helped me make the costume. She twisted the antennae just right and put perfect little silver beads on the ends.

"You're good at this, Rosemary," I told her. She blinked that suspicious blink of hers. I felt like she could see right through me. It made me a little uncomfortable.

"Will you help me with *my* costume now?" she asked. She was going to be a country music singer.

"Sure," I said. "I'll poof up your hair, and you can use the uke as a guitar."

"And lots of makeup," she added. "You know how to put on makeup, don't you, Lav?"

There was that blink again. The real Lav didn't know an eye shadow from an iPhone. Was Rosemary onto us?

I shrugged. There was nothing I could do about it, so I might as well have fun with my sister while I had one.

"I'll do your makeup," I offered. "You'll need lots of rouge, and maybe some false eyelashes."

She grinned and sat back to let me transform her into a country music diva. I had just finished teasing her hair when John arrived to pick me up. Rosemary twirled in front of him, showing off her costume, then ran off to go trick-or-treating.

John was an alien too, but his costume was nicer than mine. He was more of a sleek rock-star alien, with a lightning bolt over his eye and gold spray in his hair. He'd taken a Spider-Man costume and dyed it silver, transforming it into alien skin. Next to him I looked like the Incredible Hulk Junior. But he didn't seem to mind.

John took my hand as we walked into the gym. The Social Committee had decorated it as a haunted house, with cobwebs, witches, and ghosts hanging from the walls and a short maze of spooky dioramas to walk through. The lights were dimmed by orange gels for an eerie effect.

"Nice try," John said as we looked around. "But I can still smell the dirty gym socks."

Where were Zoe and Kelsey? It seemed strange that they hadn't arrived yet. Zoe liked to get an early start on her evil schemes.

"Want something to drink?" John asked.

I nodded. Maybe a drink would take my mind off my impending doom.

We walked over to the refreshment area. There were slices of pizza, chips, and carrot sticks at one table, and cupcakes at another table. Mr. Brummel and Madame Geller served sodas and water at the drinks table.

"Hello there, Lavender," Mr. Brummel said.

"Hi, Mr. Brummel. *Bonjour*, Madame Geller," I said. "*Comment ça va?*"

Madame Geller looked at me in surprise. "You are not in my French class, are you, dear?"

Whoops. I'd forgotten for a second that Lavender didn't speak French. "I picked up a few phrases from my friend Scarlet."

Mr. Brummel smiled. "That's very nice to hear. Something to drink?"

"Diet Coke, please," I ordered.

Now it was John's turn to be surprised. "You never struck me as a Diet Coke type," he said, asking for a root beer for himself.

True, Lavender was more of a grape soda girl. But I was tired of worrying about what made Lavender Lavender and what made me me. We were all jumbled up together now. Merging. And changing. Everyone else would have to adjust to the blur.

I shrugged. "It's what I'm in the mood for."

Mr. Brummel poured us a root beer and a Diet Coke. "Have a magical night, kids!"

"Do you want to dance?" John asked.

I shook my head. "I'm not a great dancer."

"Me either," he said. "I like to watch other people dance."

We watched the dancers. Some kids couldn't see too well out of their masks and kept bumping into people. Dragons tripped over their tails and princesses stepped on other princesses' trains.

Maybelle waved from the dance floor. She wore a Heidi costume. Ian was Frankenstein.

A few minutes later, Zoe arrived, dressed as a black cat. Kelsey was a pirate. They had masks on, but I would have known Zoe's sneaky walk anywhere. They'd come together. No dates.

Bad luck for me. Once Zoe spotted Ian with Maybelle, she'd probably get mad. And a mad Zoe was a mean Zoe.

My night was about to be ruined.

25

Cupcakes and a Candle

Charlie and I were about to go into the gym when I spied a black cat and a pirate tying a big, shaggy dog to the bike rack.

"Zoe, what are you doing?" I asked.

Zoe's wicked grin looked even wickeder surrounded by kitty-cat whiskers. "Charlie, can Scarlet meet you inside? I need to talk to her for a second. Girl stuff."

Charlie frowned and let his hair fall forward over his face. He must have been annoyed. We'd just arrived at the dance and already there was girl stuff going on.

"I'll be right in," I told him. He went inside. "What's with the dog?" I asked Zoe. "Your date for the night?"

"No." A dark look crossed her face. "I'm going inside to find Ian in a minute. This is Twinkletoes, my neighbor's dog."

"He doesn't look like a Twinkletoes," I said. "He looks more like a Grover. Or maybe a Bruno."

"The name fit him when he was a puppy," Zoe said. "He grew out of it."

"He could be a Shaggy," I said. "Or a Homer."

"Forget about his name," Zoe snapped. "Twinkletoes is part of our plan."

"What plan?" I felt queasy. "The stink spray?"

"Operation Lavender," Pirate Kelsey said. "We're entering Twinkletoes in the Costume Contest."

Every year at the Spooktacular Mr. Brummel awarded prizes for the best costumes. I couldn't see what this had to do with "Operation Lavender."

"But . . . Twinkletoes doesn't go to our school," I said. "He's not eligible for the contest. And he doesn't have a costume."

"Yes, he does." Zoe produced a cardboard sign with a ribbon attached. It said LAVENDER SCHMITZ. She hung the sign around Twinkletoes's neck.

"When Mr. Brummel asks us what Twink is supposed to be, we'll say that this is Lavender — only she forgot her costume," Zoe said. "Poor Lavender. She missed her regular appointment at Dottie's Dog-Topia and this is the sad result. More hair than a French poodle."

"We'll be sure to speak clearly into the mike so everyone will get the joke," Kelsey said.

"Lavender would have to be crazy to show her face at a dance again," Zoe said. "Costume or no costume."

I boiled with rage, but tried to control myself. "What do you have against Lavender?" I demanded. "What has she ever done to you?"

"Isn't it obvious?" Zoe said. "All you have to do is look at her. She's just . . . *wrong*."

That hurt. "What does that mean?" I really wanted to know. I'd felt that way before — that something about me seemed wrong to people like Zoe, on some gut level that no one could explain.

"What, do you like her?" Kelsey said.

"Yes," I said. "I do like her. I like Lavender."

And it was true. I knew I was talking about myself, of course, but I'd never been able to say that out loud before: I liked myself.

It felt good.

At first they were silent. I could see the confusion working on their faces. Had their friend Scarlet just admitted that she liked Lavender Schmitz? It did not compute.

"I think you like Lavender more than you like me," Zoe said.

Whoa — was Zoe . . . hurt? That caught me off guard.

"This isn't about who likes who more." I trod carefully, not wanting to upset her, but not wanting to back down either. "All I said was that I like Lavender. I like you too." A white lie, but I had to protect myself.

"No." Zoe's face hardened. "This is a loyalty test, Scarlet. Are you on my side, or Lavender's?"

"Why do I have to take sides? I can like more than one person at a time."

"Not with me you can't." Zoe patted Twinkletoes. "And so, the test. We're pranking Lavender tonight. Are you in?"

"No," I said.

"Fine." Zoe's voice cracked. "You made your choice, and now I know where I stand with you. Operation Lavender is now Operation Lavender and Scarlet. While we're pranking

Lavender, I'll remind everyone in school that *you* started this whole Dog-Topia joke. See how your friend Lavender likes that. By the end of the night, you won't have a friend in the world. Not even me."

"You and your new best friend Lavender can be outcast losers together," Kelsey said. "Except she probably won't want to talk to you."

Zoe laughed. "Snubbed by Lavender. That's about as low as you can get."

"I'll live," I said.

"You would have pranked Lavender in a second . . . *before*," Zoe said. "Before you changed."

Was that true? Would Scarlet really have done something so mean to me . . . more than once?

"Scarlet?" Zoe said. "Last chance to save yourself from utter social annihilation."

"Don't do this, Zoe," I pleaded. "This is *your* last chance. To save yourself."

"Save *my*self! I'm not in any danger. . . ."

She didn't get it. She thought people liked meanness. I had to believe she was wrong.

I guessed we were going to find out.

"I've got to go," I said. "Charlie's waiting." I went inside to find him.

"You'll be sorry!" Zoe called after me. "Don't come crying to us when all of Falls Road Middle School turns its back on you!"

The gym was dark, the music loud, and lots of kids were

dancing. Maybelle shimmied in the middle of the dance floor, waving her hands at a giant Frankenstein's monster.

Who was the monster? I moved in for a closer look. Frankenstein took Maybelle by the hand and twirled her around. Then, hot and sweaty, he pulled off his rubber mask and revealed his true identity.

Ian Colburn!

Ian Colburn? Dancing with Maybelle? Good for her!

My heart rose with joy. Maybelle had been crushing on Ian for a long time. Why hadn't she told me he'd asked her to the Spooktacular?

Then I remembered that Maybelle thought I was Scarlet. There was no reason for her to confide in me.

I felt sad. And then I felt worried.

Because Ian was supposed to be Zoe's date. At least, that was what Zoe seemed to think.

I heard the gym door open behind me and turned to see Zoe and Kelsey come in. Zoe's eyes went straight to Maybelle and Ian. Maybe I imagined it, but I could have sworn that, just for a second, they welled up with tears.

"Ian asked me to the dance, you know," Zoe informed me. "I said no."

"He's a big idiot," Kelsey added.

"Yeah, typical soccer player," Zoe sniffed. "All feet and no brains."

The DJ played a new song. Ian twirled Maybelle again, ready for another dance. He liked her. Anybody could see that.

I felt happy for Maybelle, but I felt something else too.

"You're lying," I said to Zoe. "Ian never asked you to the dance. No one asked you. No one asked either of you, did they?"

Zoe's eyes flashed. But this wasn't her usual glimmer of evil. It was a spark of pain. And there they were again: the tears. My words had hit their target. I couldn't help feeling a jolt of satisfaction.

"When did you get so mean, Scarlet?" Zoe asked.

"Mean?" I asked. "Me?"

"Yeah, you."

Well, not me, really. Scarlet. Zoe's best friend. Scarlet was the one Zoe thought was mean.

I wasn't mean to anyone. Everyone else was mean to me.

All I did was tell the truth in a sharply pointed way. That was what I'd always done. No one had ever minded before. In fact, they'd never paid much attention to what I said when I was Lavender.

But now that Zoe mentioned it, maybe I was a little mean sometimes. I'd almost made my mother cry on my birthday, hadn't I?

When Ben was mean to me, I was mean right back, at least at first.

And now I'd practically made Zoe Carter, of all people, cry.

I could be mean, just like everybody else.

Including Scarlet.

When she'd said she was sorry, I could tell she meant it.

Zoe and Kelsey stood close together, watching the dancers in their costumes. They had their secrets too, private things that made them happy and sad. I didn't particularly care to find out what they were. But the secrets were there.

Underneath their Halloween costumes, everybody was hiding something.

"You used to be my best friend, Scarlet," Zoe said with a catch in her voice. "Now you avoid me. You don't sit with me at lunch. You never text or call me. You abandoned me!"

I stared at her. "I? Abandoned *you*?"

"Everybody's abandoned me!" Zoe cried.

"What about me?" Kelsey said. "I'm your best friend too."

Zoe scowled. "I'm talking to Scarlet now." Kelsey's lip quivered.

I didn't like Zoe. But at that moment, on Halloween night, I glimpsed some fear. She was worried that as things changed, the new order wouldn't have a place for her. After I saw that fear, I couldn't hate her. I tried. I really did. I just couldn't do it.

"Get away from me, Scarlet," Zoe said. "Go find your dumb date."

"Yeah," Kelsey said. "We'll see you later — when we totally ruin you."

"Don't do it, you guys," I said one last time. "I'm telling you — you'll be sorry."

I wasn't threatening them. I was warning them. I was trying to help them. Honest.

Zoe couldn't hurt me. Once I realized I didn't need to be afraid of her, her power vanished.

Poof. Almost like magic.

She was just a girl like me.

Charlie waved to me from the refreshment table. I started toward him, and as I got closer, I noticed something strange.

A platter full of cupcakes frosted in a familiar pink icing.

And decorating the table was a large pumpkin candle molded, naturally, of orange wax.

Could that candle have possibly been made in Kalamazoo?

I stopped short, dove through the mob of dancing kids, and grabbed Scarlet.

"Lavender, hi!" she said. "Does this mean you forgive me?"

"Quiet." I dragged her to the cake table. "Look."

I picked up a cupcake and peeled back the paper. Underneath the frosting: devil's food cake.

I took a bite.

"Taste this," I said, shoving it into her mouth. "Taste familiar?"

Scarlet's eyes opened wide and she nodded. She mumbled something but I couldn't understand her because her mouth was full.

"What?" I asked.

She swallowed the cake. "Are we friends?"

"Yes," I said. "We're friends."

She smiled. I never was a big smiler, so I wasn't used to seeing my mouth twisted into that formation. But it did a lot for my face.

We shook on it. Friends.

We faced the big pumpkin candle. The flame flickered and glowed.

Scarlet tilted the candle. We ducked down to read the mark on the bottom.

"It's there," she said.

The stamp was faint. But I could just make out the words. MADE IN KALAMAZOO.

I could hardly believe it. Finally! We had a chance to reverse this spell and go back to being ourselves again!

"Please let it work," I whispered. "Please, please let it work. . . ." I turned to Scarlet and said, "This is it. You know what to do."

Scarlet nodded and took my hand. She closed her eyes. I closed mine.

"On three," I said. "Don't forget to wish."

"I'm wishing harder than I ever wished for anything in my life," she said.

"One . . . two . . . three!"

Together, we blew out the candle.

I opened my eyes and blinked.

26

The Costume Parade

I opened my eyes.

"Lavender?" I asked.

"Yes?" She stared at me.

I touched her straw hula skirt. "Is that you in there?"

Lavender touched the green paint on my face. "Yes." There was defeat in her voice. She stood before me, tall, dark-blond, hazel-eyed . . . still in my body.

"It didn't work," Lavender said.

I felt the top of my head, the alien antennae, just to be sure. They were still stuck to my thick hair. I stared at my hand. Stubby fingers.

Lavender was right. The candle hadn't worked.

"What are we going to do now?" I asked.

Mr. Brummel was working at the refreshments table. "Girls, why did you blow out the candle?" He patted his pockets, looking for a match so he could relight it.

"Sorry, Mr. B.," I said.

Mr. Brummel found a match and struck it. "Please don't blow out the candle again. This is Halloween, girls, not a birthday party." He relit the candle. The wick sparked, then glowed.

"Mr. B.," Lavender said. "That candle comes from Kalamazoo."

"Does it?" Mr. Brummel shrugged. "How do you know that?"

"It says so on the bottom," I replied. "We checked."

"That seems like an odd thing to do," Mr. Brummel said. "Checking the bottom of a candle to see where it comes from. What difference does it make to you?"

"We thought it might matter," I said. "Do you know anything about this candle, anything at all? Like how it got here?"

"Or if it has any special, um, qualities?" Lavender added.

"No," Mr. Brummel said. "It doesn't smell like pumpkins, if that's what you mean."

"But Kalamazoo is your hometown," Lavender said.

"So?" Mr. Brummel said. "You're from Baltimore, and they make spices here. Do those two facts have anything to do with each other?"

"I guess not," I said. We were groping for answers, anything that might solve our crazy problem. The whole cupcake and candle thing was beginning to seem silly.

"I've got to go up onstage now," Mr. Brummel said. "I'm judging the costume contest. Magic time."

"Magic," Lavender said. "Exactly. We need magic. . . ."

Mr. Brummel mounted the stage and took the DJ's microphone. "Attention, everyone! It's time for the Costume Contest!"

"Oh no," Lavender said. "This is going to be bad."

"I'm bracing myself," I said.

"You definitely should," Lavender said.

Charlie and John came to get us. John took my hand. "Come on, Lavender," he said. "Let's enter the contest."

"We'll never win," I said. Winning a costume contest was the last thing I cared about.

"Why not?" John said. "I think we look convincingly alien."

The four of us lined up with the others to march past Mr. Brummel and show off our costumes. I looked for Zoe, but I didn't see her anywhere. That made me nervous.

Here it comes, I thought. *Some dreadful embarrassment. Some kind of smelly thing to dump on my head, or a big five-foot-high picture of me with my skirt tucked into my underwear, or maybe a song written just for me, all about how dorky I am.*

It wouldn't be about me, really, of course, but about Lavender. Though I was having a hard time seeing where Lavender stopped and I began. The line was getting fuzzier all the time.

Zoe could ridicule Lavender, but she'd really be making fun of me. And if she went after me — Scarlet — that would hurt too.

The gym door banged open, and a tall black cat burst in, followed by a pirate. Or rather, a girl in a black cat costume, and another girl in a pirate costume. The cat was walking a big shaggy dog with a sign around its neck that said LAVENDER SCHMITZ.

Kids started laughing at the dog as Zoe marched it around the room. Some of them tried to pet it.

Hmmm . . . okay. That wasn't a dream come true, but it was also not so bad. Yet.

The dog trotted happily around the room with its tongue hanging out. *Wow*, I thought, *that dog sure is hairy.*

Hairy.

Very hairy.

Then I understood what Zoe was up to.

Lavender. The dog salon.

The nasty joke I'd made about Lavender needing to go to a dog groomer because she was so hairy.

Ugh, why had I ever made that ridiculous joke?

Zoe was going to rat me out to everyone. Lavender already knew how mean I was. Soon Maybelle and John and Charlie would know too.

I was in Lavender's body. I felt her face get red and hot. This was embarrassing for me as Lavender. But in a way it was worse for the Scarlet inside me.

Zoe paraded the dog through the crowd while kids laughed. John squeezed my hand. "Who is that?" he asked.

"Zoe and Kelsey."

"They're idiots." He squeezed my hand again. It helped.

"I know."

Zoe impatiently cut to the front of the costume parade. She wanted to make her point, get her prank in now before Mr. Brummel or some other teacher stopped her. She led the dog up onto the stage in front of Mr. Brummel.

"What are you supposed to be?" he asked. "A dog and a cat?"

Zoe grabbed the microphone from him. "Mr. Brummel, I'd like to make a public service announcement if I may."

"Can it wait until after the contest?" Mr. Brummel said.

Zoe elbowed him away. "No, it can't. This is for all you dorks out there who think Scarlet Martinez is your friend. I'm looking at you, Maybelle, and you, John, and Charlie, and especially you, Lavender Schmitz."

Zoe looked right at me. *I'm Scarlet, you twit*, I thought.

"Somebody should shut her up," John said.

"Scarlet is not the nice girl you think she is," Zoe said. "I have proof. You all should know what kind of friend Scarlet really is."

I squeezed my eyes shut. I wished so hard that I'd never said anything mean about anyone. I wished I could take it all back. I wished I could start all over again and choose new friends. I'd choose Lavender. And Maybelle. And Charlie. And John. But not Zoe.

The microphone squealed and I heard a scuffle on the stage. I opened my eyes. Lavender was up there, wresting the mike out of Zoe's hands. Mr. Brummel looked on like a ref at a boxing match.

"Get it! Get the mike!" the crowd yelled. "Go Scarlet!"

Lavender managed to snatch the mike away. The crowd cheered.

Lavender cleared her throat. "I know what Zoe's going to say. I'd like to explain."

The room went quiet.

"I once did something very mean to Lavender," she said. "She already knows all about it. She doesn't need to hear that bad old joke again."

I swallowed. What was Lavender doing?

"I'm sorry about what I did," Lavender said. "It was a mistake. I'm a different person now. I apologized to Lavender, and she forgives me. She told me so herself."

Lavender looked at me when she said that. I got the message. She forgave me.

"Isn't that nice of Lavender?" Lavender said. "She's very cool. You all really should get to know her better."

Zoe pulled the mike toward her mouth. "That wasn't what I was going to say! Scarlet's a traitor and a —"

Mr. Brummel reached between them and grabbed the mike. "Girls! Can we please get back to the costume contest?"

Defeated, Zoe and the dog left the stage and ran out of the gym. Kelsey followed.

I felt sad for Zoe. We were once best friends. I thought we were, anyway. She thought we were too.

It hurt to lose a friend. Even a friend I'd grown out of.

The costume parade continued, though no one seemed to care about it anymore. Finally it sputtered to a close.

"Before I announce the winners," Mr. Brummel said, "I'd like to remind you all that you are participating in an ancient ritual. Halloween is a chance to cast off our old workaday selves and become someone new. A creature of fantasy, whatever our fantasies may be."

While Mr. Brummel rambled on, I watched Lavender and Charlie. He held her hand. Once in a while he looked at her through his curtain of hair, as if he couldn't believe she was real. As if he couldn't believe how lucky he was to be holding her hand.

I wished I could be in her place. Back in my old body. Holding hands with Charlie. Seeing him look at me the way he was looking at her.

John put his arm around me. Lavender glanced over at us.

She wanted to trade places with me too. I could see it in her eyes.

"Halloween is a holiday of tradition and superstition, much like the theater —" Mr. Brummel said.

All of a sudden, Lavender's eyes bugged out.

She made some quick excuse to Charlie and grabbed my arm.

"I think I found the answer!" she whispered. "We're saved!"

She pulled me away from the crowd.

"Where are we going?" I asked.

"To the auditorium."

27

The Magic of the Theater

I knew I had the answer. I just knew it. I ran to the auditorium as fast as I could, dragging Scarlet behind me. "What is it?" she kept asking, while I kept wanting to say, "Run faster!" But I understood why she couldn't run faster — she was saddled with my stubby legs — and decided to be kind.

When we got there, the auditorium was locked.

"We'll have to get the key from Mr. Brummel," Scarlet said. She sat down in front of the door, out of breath.

"I'll go back to the dance and find him," I offered. "You wait here."

I jogged back to the gym, my long Scarlet legs floating me easily across the school grounds. The costume contest was over and the stage was empty. Madame Geller manned the drinks table alone.

"Have you seen Mr. Brummel?" I asked.

Madame Geller shook her head. "He disappeared a few minutes ago. Didn't say where he was going. I wish he'd come back and help me like he promised."

I searched the whole gym, but Mr. Brummel was gone.

Rats.

Scarlet was still waiting in front of the auditorium. "I couldn't find him," I reported. "He hasn't come by this way, has he?"

"No. What are we going to do?"

"I don't know. The idea I had — well, I have a feeling it will work best in the auditorium, on a real stage."

"Nothing we try ever seems to work out," Scarlet said.

"Not easily, anyway," I added.

We sat quietly for a minute, watching the red taillights of a car drift away from the gym.

"Lavender." Scarlet cleared her throat. "Why did you defend me tonight?"

"Well, I did it because . . ." Why had I defended her? It had felt right. I understood her better, how she could have gotten lost somewhere along the way. How I'd gotten lost too. How I might have gotten caught up in the same mess, in her place. "I guess because I forgive you."

"Thank you." Scarlet picked at a spot of green face paint. "If we ever do manage to switch back into our own bodies, I'm going to do things differently."

"Me too."

"For one thing, I've been hanging with the wrong people," Scarlet said. "People who don't know how to be friends. Maybelle and John — they're real friends. And Charlie too."

She was right. I'd always told myself I had no friends. But I had wonderful friends. The best kids in the school. Maybelle, John, Charlie — and Scarlet.

"I thought no one liked me because I'm not pretty like you," I said.

"Lots of people like you," Scarlet said. "Even though you're a grump half the time. Anyway, you shouldn't define yourself by your looks."

"I can't *believe* that you, of all people, are saying that to me. You're the one who's famous for being so pretty."

"Right. And what did that get me? It didn't get me friends I can trust. It didn't get me the lead in the school musical. And it didn't get me a starting spot on the soccer team — that was hard work and talent."

"You're so modest," I teased.

"I'm just saying, good looks haven't gotten me any of the things I care about most." She peeled away a little more green face paint, frowning. "Being pretty's definitely the most important thing to my mom. And she's not happy. She ended up with that blockhead Steve and that horrible zombie Ben."

"Ben's not so bad, you know."

"What? Hasn't he been insulting you? Calling you plastic-head and a pawn of the corporate conspiracy?"

"He started out that way. But he's just as unhappy at home as you are. Steve is really hard on him. At least your mother cares about you. Steve is just selfish. And Ben is lonely. Don't let Steve push you around. You and Ben could team up against him, get him to respect you more."

"Steve doesn't listen to me. And Ben deserves to be lonely. He's so mean!"

"If you try being a little bit nice to him, he's not so mean."

"Why doesn't *he* be nice to me first?"

"Because he's worse off than you. Besides, somebody has to go first."

"Well, you could be nicer to your family too," Scarlet said. "Your mom — all she wants to do is make you happy. She'll do anything! And Rosemary looks up to you, and you keep putting her down. And your dad's pretty funny, once you get used to his sense of humor."

"They're so embarrassing," I protested. "My mom would hug me twenty-four hours a day if I let her. She'd never stop! And my dad lives to mortify me."

"Yeah, but they love you, and you know it."

She was right, of course. I missed my cozy, embarrassing family. "If I ever get to live with them again, I promise to appreciate them more."

"If if if," Scarlet said. "If only we could switch back!"

"We can," I said. "I'm pretty sure I know how. But we have to get into the auditorium first."

Scarlet stood up and tried the door again, rattling it. "I'm ready to be myself now. I'm so ready!"

"Ready?" Mr. Brummel stepped out of the shadows. "What are you two doing out here?"

I jumped to my feet. "We've been looking for you, Mr. B.! Can you let us into the auditorium?"

"I've got the keys. If you left something in there, I can get it for you —"

"It's not that," I said. "It's —" How to explain?

"We were so inspired by the speech you gave at the Spooktacular," Scarlet jumped in, "that we wanted to rehearse on our own, right now."

"That's right," I said. "Lavender's going to practice her songs, and I'm going to listen."

"Well, I guess that's okay," Mr. Brummel said. "It's kind of nice, actually. Do you need help with the lights?"

He unlocked the door and let us in, switching on the houselights. Then he disappeared backstage. After a few seconds, two spotlights illuminated the stage.

We'd told him that Lavender wanted to practice her songs. How did he know we needed two spotlights?

"I'll be back later to lock up." He hopped off the stage and started out the door. "Have fun!" He switched off the house-lights on his way out, so that the spotlights on the stage were the only illumination.

Scarlet and I stood on the dark stage in the silent theater, hovering between the two spotlights.

"Okay, Lavender. He's gone. What's your plan?"

"When Mr. B. said *theater* and then *superstition*, it reminded me of that rhyme he taught us," I said. *"Know the role you want to play and say the name three times this way —"*

"Backward and forward and so on," Scarlet said. "I did that rhyme."

"So did I."

We looked at each other.

"Maybe," I said. "The cake and the candle didn't work — at least, not by themselves. Maybe we need to add the chant too. Let's try it again. Only this time, say the name of the person you want to be now. Who do you want to be more than anyone else in the world?"

"Scarlet Martinez."

"And I want to be Lavender Schmitz."

"So I say my own name? And you say your own name?" I nodded.

"Do you really think it will work?" Scarlet asked.

"Who knows?" I said. "Do you have any other ideas?"

"No," she admitted. "Let's try it."

"Maybe the rhyme will have more power if we chant it at the same time," I said. "Together."

"Okay."

"You take stage right and I'll take stage left."

I moved into the spotlight on stage right. Scarlet stood in the light on stage left. We looked at each other across the boards. She nodded. It was time to begin.

We chanted:

Know the role you want to play

And say the name three times this way:

backward, forward,

upward, downward,

inward, outward,

eastward, westward,

northward, southward,

most of all, heavenward.

"Redneval, Redneval, Redneval," I recited. "Lavender, Lavender, Lavender."

I said my own name upward, downward, inward, outward, eastward, westward, northward, southward.

I heard Scarlet on the other side of the stage, chanting her own name the way I chanted mine.

Then I clasped my hands together in the most fervent prayer and looked toward heaven. The spotlight bleached my vision.

"Lavender Lavender Lavender!" I pleaded.

"Scarlet Scarlet Scarlet!" Scarlet shouted.

The names echoed through the theater, then faded away to silence.

We waited.

Suddenly the spotlights went out. The auditorium was dark.

"Help!" Scarlet cried. "Someone turned off the lights!"

"I've got it." I groped my way backstage to the light board and flicked a switch. The stage lights came on, just one big flood of light.

I looked across the stage at Scarlet. She stared at me with her big hazel eyes.

Scarlet's eyes. Not mine.

She was wearing a hula outfit, tall and athletic with dark-blond hair.

Shaking, I held up my hand. It was coated with green body paint.

Because Lavender was an alien for Halloween.

And I was Lavender again!

"It worked!" Scarlet squealed. "It worked! We're back!"

"We're back!" I cried. I grabbed her hands and we jumped up and down, squealing. Just like I used to see her do with Zoe. But this was different. This was real happiness. And real friendship.

We went back to the gym to find John and Charlie. They were wandering around looking for us.

"I get Charlie now, right?" Scarlet whispered.

"And I get John," I said.

"Right."

The boys ran to us. John took my hand. "Where did you go? Are you okay?"

"I'm fine," I told him. "I just needed some air."

"That was a lot of air. Were you upset?" he asked. "About Zoe's joke?"

"Not really," I said. "I just wasn't feeling like myself. But I'm all better now."

He grinned. "Good. Want to dance?"

"Sure."

A slow song started. John put his arms around me. I felt my wide feet clomp on the floor. I stepped on John's foot. He didn't seem to mind.

Ah. Back to my clumsy old self.

It felt good.

28

Showdown

Mom was waiting up for me in the kitchen when Charlie dropped me home after the dance. I threw my arms around her neck and kissed her. She smelled sweet, like vanilla perfume.

"Hi, honey!" She seemed surprised at how excited I was to see her. "How was the dance?"

"So good." Once I'd gotten my not-so-clumsy body back, I was itching to dance. So Lavender, John, Maybelle, Ian, Charlie, and I danced until the very last song. Mr. Brummel practically had to kick us out of the gym. Then Charlie walked me home, holding my hand the whole way.

"Tell me all about it," she said.

"It started out a little rocky. They had a costume contest. . . ." I gave her a highly edited version of the evening, mostly focusing on the last part, when my friends and I made a big circle and chorus-line-kicked to every song the DJ played. She squeezed my hand while I talked.

This is making her so happy, I thought. *And all I'm doing is talking to her.*

Steve came in for a glass of water, wearing his bathrobe. "Home at last, I see. Don't you have a ten o'clock curfew?"

"I got home at ten," I told him.

"So why haven't you come to bed yet, Leigh?"

"Scarlet was telling me about the dance," Mom said.

"That's fine, but now it's time to come to bed." He left the room.

"We both should go to bed. Come on, Scarlet." Mom led me upstairs and kissed me good night outside of my room. "I'm glad you had a good time."

It felt good to be home. Back to my big, comfortable room, which Lavender had left in a mess. I changed out of my hula costume and into my pajamas, straightening things up as I went. I could hear Ben through the wall, playing *Skullmuncher 7*. I went out and knocked on his door.

"Go away," Ben called.

"It's me, Scarlet."

Normally that would make him yell "Go away" even louder. But I remembered what Lavender had told me — that he was lonely — and thought I'd see for myself.

He opened the door. "Yeah?"

"Ben, I've been thinking." I stepped into his room and shut the door behind me, a bold move the old Scarlet never would have dared.

And he protested, right on schedule. "Hey, what are you —?"

"We need to make some changes around here, starting with the way Steve treats us," I said, interrupting him. "Both of us. Are you in?"

Ben looked confused at first, but then he grinned.

"What did you have in mind?" he asked.

"Here she comes, Queen of the Shopping Mall," Steve said when I came down for breakfast the next morning. I wasn't wearing anything unusual, just my favorite jeans and a blue top with silver threads knitted through it. "Flashier than a disco ball. Where are you off to today — out to spend more of my money?"

I refused to let him get to me. The old Scarlet would have cowered or sulked, like Mom did. Not anymore. "Actually, I'm going to go over to my friend Lavender's to practice for the musical."

"I thought you didn't get a part, sweetie," Mom said.

"I'm in the chorus," I said. "The chorus is important too."

"The chorus is for the no-talents, right, Ben?" Steve looked to Ben, expecting support. But he wasn't going to get it.

I hoped.

Ben just stirred his Coco Puffs till the milk turned brown.

That didn't stop Steve. "I keep telling you, Scarlet — stick to what you're good at. Of course, some people aren't good at much of anything. I'm still waiting for Ben to figure out what talent he's got besides loafing around."

"He's good at playing games," I said. I was determined to stick up for Ben, whether he stuck up for me or not.

"I mean something worthwhile," Steve said.

"Ben's good at a lot of things," I said. I didn't know what they were, but there had to be something he could do well. "That isn't the point."

Steve stared at me with an infuriating, amused smile on his face. "Oh, and what *is* the point, Scarlet? I'd like to hear this."

"The point is . . ." My voice started shaking. Steve was intimidating. "The point is, you're Ben's father, and my stepfather, and you shouldn't talk to us this way."

"What way?"

"Disrespectfully. As if everything we say and do is stupid or wrong. Ben and I are unhappy and we want to see some changes around here. Right, Ben?"

"Right." Ben abandoned his Coco Puffs to stand beside me.

"It hurts when you put us down," I told Steve. "Just because our interests are different from yours, that doesn't make them less worthy."

Steve laughed in disbelief. "Talk about disrespectful. Leigh, do you hear how your daughter is speaking to me?"

"I have a right to voice my opinion," I insisted.

Mom's eyes were wide. She looked from me to Steve without saying anything. I knew she felt torn, and I didn't expect much help from her. It would have been nice, though.

"Yeah, you think your opinion is the only one that counts, because you earn the money for the family," Ben said. "But you care about money too much. You should care about my feelings sometimes. And Scarlet's."

"And mine," Mom said. She stood up with me and Ben now, the three of us facing Steve like a brick wall.

"Yeah, and Mom too!" I put my arm around her, so happy that she was finally sticking up for herself, and for me.

"Sit down, Leigh," Steve said. "You're not helping."

"The kids are right, Steve," Mom said. "You could have more respect for all of us. From now on, we're going to demand it."

Steve tried to hide it, but I could tell he was nervous now that he was outnumbered. "Leigh. Ben. Scarlet. My family. Come on. Let's settle down now. Be reasonable. I care about all of you. I'm only trying to encourage you to be the best people you can be."

"We're trying to help you too, Dad," Ben said. "You could be a better father. I'm telling you how."

"And a better stepfather, and a better husband," Mom added.

His resistance was weakening. We'd gotten to him.

"From now on, we all get a say in what happens in this house," I declared.

"And we will all treat one another with respect," Mom said. "Or you'll have a mutiny on your hands."

Steve hesitated. I thought he was afraid of giving up his power. But maybe he was beginning to see that he'd never really had much power in the first place. And he had very little left now.

"All right," he said at last. "I'm sorry. I didn't realize I was hurting you all so much. From now on, I'll try to do better. But I might need a little reminder once in a while."

"Don't worry," I said. "We'll be happy to remind you."

29

At Long Last, Scrapple

"Lavender, want to go shopping today? A little shopping, a little lunch?"

Mom looked hopeful, as if she expected me to say yes to that question. And then I remembered where she'd gotten the idea that I'd gladly go shopping — from Scarlet, who had conspired with my mother to add a few new clothes to my weirdly neat room. There was even makeup, which I doubted I'd use. Although I had been successful at putting my new contact lenses in. I didn't mind not having glasses.

But Mom looked so excited I couldn't say no. A little shopping wouldn't kill me. "Can we go to Ma Petite Shoe?" I asked. It was the best kind of shoe store — the kind that also sold chocolate.

"All right, if you promise to try on at least one pair of shoes."

"Deal," I said. "Want to come, Rosemary?"

"Shopping again?" Dad thoughtfully chewed on a slice of bacon. "What, did you grow out of last week's clothes already?"

"We're building a wardrobe, Frank," Mom said. "We're just

getting started. And don't worry — we're not spending a lot of money. We're being very choosy."

Dad shrugged. "I don't see the point. It makes no difference what you wear, Lavender. You always look beautiful to me."

"Aw, Dad." I kissed him on the forehead. The kitchen went silent. That "aw" was a clear signal that the Lavender they once knew was gone.

And yet, she wasn't. I was back, the real Lavender. I'd just changed a lot in the last few days.

Rosemary — who, with her freaky radar, seemed to sense that something uncanny was happening — studied me through her thick glasses, ready to pounce on any sign that I wasn't the old Lavender. I was about to ask, "What are you blinking at, Rabbit-face?" but the snark got caught in my throat. I remembered Ben, and Scarlet's mom, and Steve — the family I had almost been stuck with forever — and a surge of grateful warmth for Mom and Dad and Rosemary flooded through me. They were my family, they loved me, and yes, I loved them too. I wouldn't have been comfortable with anyone else.

"What's everybody staring at?" I scooted my chair in close to the table. "Is there any scrapple in the house? I've been craving scrapple like crazy."

"But Lavender, a few days ago you said you hated scrapple," Detective Rosemary said.

Scarlet had made a few changes that were good, but others needed to be undone immediately. "Never, Rosemary. I'll love scrapple till the day I die. And if you ever hear me say I don't like it, you'll know I've been possessed by the spirit of a picky eater and am not my true self."

That freaked her out so much she dropped her fork. "I knew it," she muttered, but no one paid any attention, thank goodness.

30

Everything Old Is New Again

"All right, chorus," Mr. Brummel said. "Let's run through 'Trouble' one more time."

Monday afternoon, back at school after the Spooktacular, back in my good old Scarlet Martinez body. Also back to my Scarlet Martinez voice, unfortunately. At the beginning of rehearsal that day I tried to sing quietly, but Mr. B. scolded me.

"The chorus represents the townspeople, and not all townspeople are good singers," Mr. Brummel said. "I like the chorus to have an edge to it. So all of you shy singers, I want to hear your voices. Sing out! That means you, Scarlet Martinez."

Charlie chose that moment to pull back his curtain of hair and give me an encouraging smile. We were all in this musical together, from the stars to the stage crew. If Mr. B. needed me to sing out, then I'd sing out.

I'd wandered through school in a happy daze all day. It felt strange to be myself again. Everything was the same, but different too. I had new friends, like Lavender and Maybelle and John. I stopped by Lavender's locker to say hi in the morning, and she and Maybelle and I hung out in the hall together when we had breaks. That was different, in a nice way.

Zoe and Kelsey huddled together by themselves, quieter than usual. I knew that wouldn't last long. Zoe would be trying to run the school again in no time. But I'd be surprised if she dared to try any of her old tricks. We wouldn't let her get away with that anymore.

I was back to my old form at soccer practice. The one thing I missed was rehearsing with Charlie. Lavender looked like she was having so much fun with him onstage.

She must have read my mind, because after rehearsal she found me and said, "Don't worry. Those stage kisses aren't real."

"How did you know what I was thinking?" I asked.

"Because I know you," she said. "And you know me."

She was right: Nobody knew me like Lavender did. And nobody knew her like I did. Inside and out. Backward and forward. Upward and downward . . . the bad and the good.

That, I decided, was the best kind of friend.

31

Opening Night

Six weeks later, under the watchful eye of Don Ho, I stood center stage with Charlie and took my bows. *The Music Man* was a smashing success.

I loved being onstage and singing. I loved being Marian, and I loved being me.

The rest of the cast joined us onstage. As we clasped hands, I peeked down the chorus line at Scarlet, who was glowing.

The audience rose to its feet, cheering. Mom and Dad and Rosemary clapped and whistled in the front row. A few rows back Scarlet's mother beamed with pride, while Ben and Steve cheered for Scarlet. Ben wore a T-shirt that said GO PRINCESS P.

My time as Scarlet didn't turn me into a supercool girl. I went right back to being my same old schlubby self. Though I did start washing my hair more often. And I felt less lonely. My list of friends was getting long, and growing.

As William Shakespeare said: All's well that ends well.

The curtain fell and rose again for another ovation. John brought me a bouquet of flowers he'd folded himself.

It was the best night of my life.